MEN'S ADVENTURE READER

FROM THE CO-EDITOR OF
MEN'S ADVENTURE QUARTERLY

NUMBER ONE

TABLE OF CONTENTS

THE CANNIBAL BRIDE OF CHIEF PETTY OFFICER MOREY
By: Nathan S. Lavine Art by: Unknown
From: **MAN TO MAN,** January, 1965
08

BEAUTIES FOR THE NAZI ARTIST OF AGONY
By: Jim McDonald Art by: Unknown
From: **MAN'S BOOK,** April, 1967
22

HITLER'S BABOON TORTURES IN MABUTI
By: Harris Creeg Art by: Unknown
From: **MAN'S DARING,** January, 1962
32

UP TO MY NECK IN LIVE LOBSTERS
By: Josh Lewitt Art by: Unknown
From: **MAN'S LIFE,** July, 1957
44

LOVE IN A SUITCASE
Confessions of a Convention Queen
By: Marie Nolan Art by: Unknown
From: **MAN'S LIFE,** July, 1957
56

THE TATTOO GANG'S VICIOUS FIRE TORTURE OF THE SOCIETY DEBS
By: Kenneth Seward Photos by: Unknown
From: **MAN'S PERIL,** January, 1965
74

LOVE ME TO DEATH The Incredible Revenge of Colorado Katie
By: Dean W. Ballenger Art by: Unknown
From: **MAN'S STORY,** August, 1968
90

MY WILD ESCAPE FROM THE MAFIA'S ORGY ISLAND PARADISE

By: Bart Handley as told to Mark Brand
Art by: Norman Saunders
From: **MAN'S STORY,** December, 1973

98

DEATH WATCH OF THE 2ND PLATOON

By: Sgt. Wayne Stevens Photos by: Unknown
From: **KEN FOR MEN,** May, 1957

118

THE LAST RIDE OF THE REBEL JOY GIRL CAVALRY

By: Chuck McCarthy Art by: Unknown
From: **MAN'S STORY,** February, 1963

130

FEATURING

CLAIRE SHAW   **50**

NICKI GIBSON, VALERIE ALLEN, BONNIE BENTLEY   **63**

JUDY CROWDER: BLONDE OF THE MONTH   **112**

DAWN RICHARDS, BEVERLY NEALE   **140**

COVER: Cover art from REAL, January, 1956 by Rico Tomaso

MEN'S ADVENTURE READER is a paperback dedicated to reprinting stories, artwork, articles, and photographs from men's adventure magazines published in the 1950s, 1960s and 1970s. All contents are either in the public domain to the best of our knowledge or included through reprint agreements made with the original creators or their heirs or estates.

If you have comments or questions about the content of the **MAR**, or if you believe and can verify that something infringes on an existing copyright you hold, please email us at
cinexploits@gmail.com.

Editor & Graphic Designer
Bill Cunningham

A Pulp 2.0 Design by Bill Cunningham
Twitter: @madpulpbastard
Facebook: Facebook.com/pulp2ohpress
www.pulp2ohpress.com

MEN'S ADVENTURE READER No.1 is copyright © 2022 by Bill Cunningham and Pulp 2.0. All rights reserved.

INTRODUCTION

Welcome to the first issue of **Men's Adventure Reader**, an offshoot of its big brother **Men's Adventure Quarterly**. This paperback is an experiment of sorts to bring more readers to the men's adventure stories and their creators by giving them a sampler. So, if the **Quarterly** is a full course meal, then think of the **Reader** as the appetizer.

Back in the 1970s the men's adventure magazines were beginning their retreat from the newsstands, and their style of pulse-pounding genre fiction was being taken over by digests and true crime magazines. These digests were like the MAMs only stripped down - color covers, fewer illustrations, but with that essential element that made every MAM a must-read - *great stories*.

In addition to the digests, publishers and writers also migrated over to the 'paperback anthology' experience. Active since the 1950s, the anthologies we usually edited by a name genre writer centered on a common theme. **The DAW SF anthologies**, **The Isaac Asimov Worlds of Science Fiction**, and in a bit of irony **The Best of Fantasy & Science Fiction Magazine** were some of the best names in the anthology game. Again, these paperbacks focused on the essential element - great stories.

We've had great success with the **MAQ** in restoring and re-presenting the men's adventure magazine experience. We've had the pleasure of introducing new readers to terrific stories, the finest in commercial illustration, and the background history of all the characters and companies that went into creating the men's adventure experience. We're proud that you have responded in such an overwhelmingly positive fashion...but there was always that nagging feeling in the back of my collective head. Are we doing enough to reach out to new readers? Are we being "Johnny Appleseed" enough to get these fun stories into new hands?

In situations like this, I often turn to our Amazon reviews (*and you thought those didn't mean anything!*) and listen to our readers - what do they like? Dislike? *Ignore completely?* Then I read a comment to the effect that we should strip out all of the fancy-schmancy art and focus on more stories.

Hmmm... now that was an interesting idea!

So here it is - our little experiment that's a stripped down, black & white only, low cost volume packed with ten or more stories taken directly from the magazines. We have come up with a pulpy magazine cocktail that includes the stories, the ads, and the dames. All the things you like to "read." We hope that the MAR will fulfill its purpose in giving our audience the kind of raw, unfiltered entertainment that was the hallmark of the men's adventure magazines - war, crime, sex, treasure hunting, mountaineering, westerns, espionage, prison - all the different genres that quickened the pulse and turned the pages faster and faster.

Ladies and gentlemen, I present the first issue of the **Men's Adventure Reader**. A fun bit of publishing that hopes to be another way for you to discover the wonders and excitement of the men's adventure magazines.

Enjoy!

Bill Cunningham
Editor

THE CANNIBAL BRIDE OF CHIEF PETTY OFFICER MOREY

By: Nathan S. Lavine
Art by: Unknown
From: **MAN TO MAN,** January, 1965

Glen had a choice: accept this tasty Wallalua dish as his bride - or become the main dish for dinner

The Seahawk-a lilting name for a clumsy wooden hull boat-wallowed into New Guinea's Tanahmerah Bay an hour after dawn. Glen Nichols, QM1/c, looked at the Wallaluas on the beach. "The fat one with the green necklace is probably Kamekula," he said, extending the binoculars to Chief Petty Officer Glen Morey. "Apparently the whole came down to see him off."

Morey looked at the Wallaluas and at burly Lyle Wallace, the Australian constable who would function as interpreter during the evacuation of the Wallaluas to Port Darwin. Then he looked at the Wallalua maiden who had been swimming and who hadn't gotten around to put her sporran back on. He looked at her for a long time—he had never seen a more alluring girl.

He and Boatswain's Mate Earl Huston lowered the boat's gig and rowed ashore. "We'd better load up right away," Wallace said after he greeted the Americans. "The Japs may be closer than we think."

"OK," Morey said, lighting a cigarette. "Tell Kamekula and his family to get into the gig and we'll shove off."

"Kam's family couldn't get into that little boat," Wallace said, looking at the gig, ``if we packed 'em in with a shoehorn."

"For Pete's sake," Morey said, appraising the Wallaluas. "How many of them are his family?"

"They all are."

Morey looked incredulously at the big Australian. "The little stud's got nine wives," Wallace explained, "and each of them has at least a dozen kids."

Morey looked back at the Kamekula family. "The Seahawk," he

mumbled, "couldn't haul even half that outfit." His brow furrowed as he contemplated the problem of evacuating this enormous family. "We'll have to shuttle-run to some island," he said, "then go to Darwin for fuel -meanwhile taking as much of the family as we have room for, come back with the fuel and take the rest to a closer island, and so on until we get them all to Darwin."

"How you do it is up to you, Yank," Wallace said. "But let's get them out of here as fast as we can. The Japs would give a pretty penny to lay hands on old Kam and his brood."

Minutes later Kamekula, his five youngest wives and thirty-one offspring were on the Seahawk. "Get underway!" Morey snapped to Nichols, who was studying a chart of the region's waters. He had become irritable. Children were all over the boat; when he'd gone to the head a moment earlier a dozen of them had crowded in to see what was going on.

Nichols steered the Seahawk in a parabola past Japanese - occupied Wahke then set a straight course for Japan, southernmost of the Schlouten islands.

Interminable hours and two voyages later the Seahawk brought the last of Kamekula's proliferate family to Japen island. "I'm going ashore and stretch my legs then come back here and crawl in the sack," Morey said wearily.

He and Nichols rowed the gig ashore. Kamekula was waiting. He began a harangue. "He says he is grateful that you are saving him and his family from the vengeance of the Japanese," Wallace interpreted. "He also says that in appreciation he is offering you and your men his prettiest daughters and that the rescue will compensate for the pigs and other gifts he would normally expect for these girls."

"Naturally I wouldn't mind shacking up with these girls," Morey said, grinning, "but I'm certainly not going to marry one of them. Tell Kam thanks but..."

"I wouldn't advise insulting him by rejecting his own daughters," Wallace said. "These lads can be ugly beyond belief. Besides the risk of becoming the entree at a Wallalua banquet you'd be losing the old boy's good will, which is the reason we're rescuing him."

Morey took his first comprehensive look at Kamekula's adult daughters. "Lord ..." he mumbled. He could not even have imagined such exquisite blooms of femininity. They were physically characterized by short height, curvaceous figures, oval faces, mischievous black eyes and coffee-with-cream skin pigmentation. They wore orchids in their wavy black hair. Their only garments were palm frond sporrans which didn't conceal very much. "They're the sexiest looking dolls I've ever seen," Morey said, turning back to Wallace, "and a man would have to be a Section 8 to refuse to love them. But marriage—even by a kookie jungle ceremony -might lead to complications. Like being stuck with a zombie wife."

"Yank," Wallace said, "I'm not trying to loop you into this thing. But we're in a situation in which the consequences could be ruddy awful. Since it would be so much more pleasant to love these girls than to be eaten by them, I fail to see why you're so reluctant."

Morey looked at Kamekula's warrior sons. They were armed with siks (spears) and topepaks (bows and arrows). These weapons couldn't cope with the grease guns in the Seahawk. But, Morey worried, killing the people he had been ordered to rescue would be even tougher to explain at ComSoPac than marrying into them.

He looked at the girls again. If he had to marry one of these Stone Age maidens he would choose the one named Tinuk. "All right," he said, looking back at Wallace. "We'll go ahead with it."

KAMEKULA performed the wedding ceremony five minutes later. After a nuptial feast in which the principal food was gecko—a tropical lizard-Tinuk pantomimed with unmistakable gestures that she was ready to consummate the marriage.

Red-faced, Morey got up and went with Tinuk into the jungle. When they came to a moonlit glade carpeted with golden wattles, a species of acacia, Tinuk jerked off her sporran and flung it aside.

Later Morey lit a recuperatory cigarette and looked at the sleeping little Wallalua. Maybe, he reflected, this assignment-which he had cursed from the beginning, wouldn't be as melancholy as he had anticipated.

After a short nap Tinuk woke refreshed, bounded up giggling and seized Morey by the hand. She jabbed a finger toward the ocean and pantomimed swimming, "Why not?" Morey grinned. "I still have a little strength yet."

They plunged in and swam for the gig. "Come on in," he said, "we'll go for a spin." Morey climbed aboard, and then heard an ominous whine over his left shoulder. He turned and saw the Zero swooping down from the blue. "We've got company," he said.

He tumbled overboard, grabbed Tinuk's hand and dragged her under. When they cautiously surfaced near the boat, the whine was already vanishing in the distance.

"Must be on a recon patrol," Morey said, relieved. "Come on, let's go back before they puncture that lovely cannibal hide."

The evacuation of the Wallaluas-a Dani speaking Papuan tribe who lived in the rain forests on the northern slope of New Guinea's Orange Range-had its inception in the geographic fact that New Guinea was the lower terminus of a curving but tottering Japanese offense line which extended west of the Aleutians in the north to the Marshall islands in the east.

In support of the southern terminus the Japanese had established two main airfields: Lae and Salamaua, both in eastern New Guinea. On September 5, 1943 Lae was invaded by American forces. Seven days later Salamaua was seized.

Of the principal Japanese defenses in New Guinea, now only Hollandia remained. ComSoPac's planning staff began immediately to prepare for its invasion as a joint operation on the biggest scale yet attempted in the Pacific.

But even under the most propitious circumstances Hollandia would be tough to crack. Japanese troops were here in strength. Four Japanese airfields were in the vicinity: Hollandia, Cyclops, Sentani, and Geelvink Bay. Imperial Navy units lurked in the coves and lagoons of nearby islands. To learn as much as possible about these defenses ground patrols were ferreted into the region to supplement aerial reconnaissance.

One of these patrols-17 men of the U.S. 32nd Division was scouting southwest of Hollandia February 3, 1944. At noon a scout of the 114th Imperial External Security Brigade discovered the Americans. He ran back to the 114th's HQ and told Major Iteroki, the commandant, of his discovery. Immediately Iteroki ordered Captain Sigo Uremoto and 43 crack riflemen to stalk the Americans.

During the transpiration of these events Kamekula and about 20 warriors were hunting in the jungle. They had heard the Americans and, concealed in foliage, had watched them plod by less than 15 feet away. They had considered killing them but had decided against it because it was rumored that these big white men were enemies of the Japanese, whom they despised.

Several minutes later they discovered Uremoto and his men slinking in the direction the Americans had gone. "Let's kill them," Kamekula whispered, "before they harm the white men."

The Wallaluas, whose origins are shrouded in antiquity, were warriors of aggressive behavior and they endorsed Kamekula's suggestion with enthusiasm. Killing the Japanese, who had conscripted hundreds of Wallaluas into slave labor, would be a humanitarian diversion from the Kaku—their traditional enemies.

Moments later black eucalypti arrows hurtled out of the foliage and plunged into Uremoto's troops. "Sweep the jungle at ankle level!" the little officer bellowed. He swung his Nambu toward the concealed Wallaluas. But before he could fire Kamekula threw a sik (spear). It hurtled through his neck, impaling him to a brushbox tree. The surviving Japanese stared, terrified, at their gurgling officer, then sprinted toward the jungle. Two reached it. The others died with Wallalua arrows between their shoulders.

The Americans, alerted by screams of the dying Japanese, came to investigate. "Thanks, Mac," burly M/Sgt. Herbert McFarland said to Kamekula.

Unfortunately for Kamekula, one of the Japanese who had escaped—Sergeant Nakupo Shimabaru-was watching this dialogue from the shelter of a clump of ferns. Cursing bitterly because he had flung his Nambu aside in his anxiety to escape the arrows, he crept toward the 114th Brigade's HQ.

"The chief who ambushed us," he said to Major Iteroki, "has a scar on the left side of his face extending from ear to mouth. He has no right ear and he wears a bone in the septum of his nose."

"We will teach that perfidious barbarian the folly of collaborating with Americans!' Major Iteroki said bitterly.

The subsequent search for Kamekula was observed by Wallalua scouts of an American patrol. The Americans relayed this information to ComSoPac who decided to evacuate the old chief and his family... his sympathies for the Americans and his influence with the Wallaluas might be useful when the invasion of Hollandia was launched.

Twenty-seven year old Chief Boatswain's Mate Glen Morey, a former Akron, Ohio, resident with nine years of Navy experience, was ordered to evacuate the Kamekula family. Because Kamekula's value to the Americans was nebulous and because of preparations for the Hollandia campaign, Morey was assigned an Australian Coastal Patrol boat which had been retired in 1937 but which had been returned to duty after the beginning of hostilities-a plodding, ugly old craft whose name "Seahawk" seemed burlesque.

With a crew of three Morey sailed for Port Darwin the evening of February 8, 1944. He had never been more dejected. This was a mission of tertiary importance; he considered his designation as its commandant evidence that ComSoPac held him in low esteem.

Six days later he married Kamekula's daughter Tinuk, a development no one could have anticipated.

The morning after his wedding night, though debilitated by Tinuk's demands, he prepared to return to Port Darwin to obtain fuel to shuttle Kamekula's family to an island closer to Australia. "We have room for thirty of the Wallaluas," Morey said to Constable Wallace. "Tell Kam to designate the ones he wants to go with us."

After Kamekula learned that it would be several weeks before his family would be reunited he refused to permit their separation. "Tell him if we take a load now it will reduce the next island hop by one trip." Morey said to Wallace.

This failed to alter the little chief's decision. Disgusted, Morey and his men climbed into the gig and rowed to the Seahawk. Soon it was wallowing toward Australia.

"ComSoPac is going to raise hell about making this trip without hauling a load of zombies," Morey worried, looking back at the Wallaluas.

This was prophetic. Navy Captain Robert J. Ingelis, Commandant of Special Assignments, was infuriated. "Of all the goddam stupidity ..." he said, "bringing a third of those people now and a third next time would have reduced your overall time at least twelve days plus saving hundreds of gallons of fuel. Why didn't you tell Kamekula it had to be done your way!"

"You don't tell that cocky little son of a bitch anything, sir," Morey said dejectedly. "He tells you."

The next morning the Seahawk, drums of fuel lashed to her deck, began the long voyage to Japan -1400 miles, much of it near islands occupied by Japanese air and naval units.

The voyage was made without incident and the Seahawk anchored in the cove on Japen at noon of the fourth day. Tinuk embraced Morey the moment he climbed out of the gig, then pantomimed that she wanted to love. "Not now," Morey said. He pushed her away and went to Wallace. "Tell Kam we're loading at dawn," he said.

"Now ..." Tinuk said after Morey finished a meal of jungle fruits.

"All right," Morey said. He got up and took Tinuk's hand and went with her into the jungle.

At dawn Wallace and the Navy men designated 42 Wallaluas and ordered them to swim to the Seahawk and climb aboard.

Morey took them to Roemberpon, an island in Geelvink Bay. This was a short trip but the voyage to Waigo, the next non-Jap occupied island, would involve skirting the Vogelkop (Bird's Head), the oddly conformed northwest end of New Guinea, which was a Japanese air and naval outpost. Since it would be folly to make this cruise in daylight hours it would be done at night-and Waigo was a full night's cruise from Roemberpon.

It was dusk when the third and final trip was completed. "I for one," engineman Henry Kurtz, said wearily, "am going to be damn glad when we get this outfit to Darwin."

Morey didn't reply. He was looking at Tinuk. Tonight, he reflected, he would love her just once ... he had to be alert during the perilous journey to Waigo.

He ordered the first contingent aboard the Seahawk at dusk the next night. Then he began the voyage around Vogelkop (200 miles).

It was hazardous. There was the possibility that Japanese search planes would bomb them. Or that they would be pirated by a Japanese destroyer.

But nothing happened and they arrived at Waigo in the first light of dawn. Immediately Nichols took the Seahawk up a jungle river and anchored under overhanging trees.

"I wish ..." Morey said a little later, "that I'd brought Tinuk." Swimming with her, and loving her, would occupy the endless hours until dusk, he said.

OUR interminable nights later the last T of the Wallaluas arrived at Waigo. "Tomorrow at dusk," Morey said to Wallace, "we're shoving off for another load of fuel. We'll be back here about ..."

He didn't say the rest. Kamekula and four of his oldest sons prodded Earl Huston out of the jungle. Morey and Wallace got up and went to them. "He loved Kam's youngest wife," Wallace said, interpreting the chief's sputtering diatribe. "And Kam demands that you execute him for this violation of tribal ethics. If you don't he says he'll do it."

"Lord ..." Morey mumbled. He glared at Huston. "You moron," he said, "what were you thinking of ... your own woman is more than you can take care of!"

"Reproaching this lad won't solve the immediate problem," Wallace said grimly. "These little beggars are beastly when it comes to loving somebody else's woman."

Morey chewed pensively on his cigar. "I've got it!" he said, turning to Wallace. "Tell Kam that for so grievous a crime the officials in Australia will demand the privilege of executing Huston themselves."

Wallace told this to Kamekula. "He wants to know how they will execute him," Wallace said.

"They'll ... uh... pull him apart with four boats."

Kamekula began to grin. "He says that will be all right," Wallace interpreted.

Morey took Huston to the Seahawk and locked him in the food compartment. "I'll sit out here the rest of the day with the grease gun," he said, "in case the zombies charge their minds."

The Wallaluas, intrigued by the execution which awaited Huston, did not attempt to molest him and at dusk Morey hauled up the Seahawk's anchor.

After the wallowing boat was out of the Wallaluas' sight Morey released Huston. "Naturally," he said, "you're going to have to be replaced when we get to Darwin. And they'll probably bust you a couple pay grades."

"Okay! Okay!" Huston said shakily, still unnerved by realization that he had almost become the "long pig" at a Dani banquet.

A coxswain' named Floyd Boss was assigned to the Seahawk to replace Huston.

He was a vivacious youth. Intrigued by his new shipmates' accounts of Wallalua love, he could hardly wait to get to Waigo.

"Did they execute Huston?" Kamekula demanded the moment Morey went ashore.

"Of course," Morey said. He described this fictitious incident.

"It must have been interesting," Kamekula said, wishing he could have witnessed it.

"It was," Morey said, winking at Wallace.

Morey took the Wallaluas to Misool island. Then to Trangan, a harrowing day and night voyage which had to be made the usual three times. "The war," Morey muttered during the last of these tedious trips, "will be over before we get this outfit to Australia."

The following morning the Seahawk departed for Darwin. "I certainly don't regret," Morey said, "that this is the last trip for fuel."

A new worry arose during the second day of the return to Trangan. The skies became cumulo-nimbus clouds. This is a monsoonal region and February March are the months in which dreadful storms prevail. "Break out your life jackets," Morey said to his men. "This boat won't stand much of a storm."

The skies cleared before morning. But Morey was greeted at Trangan by an even more distressing development. "There are Japs on this island," Wallace said. "An air outfit of some kind. One of Kam's lads discovered it three days ago."

"I wonder if they saw us come in," Morey said, suddenly apprehensive.

"I doubt it... you'd know about it by now."

Morey lit a cigarette and inhaled deeply while he considered the measures this situation would demand. "Take me where I can see what they've got," he said, flinging the cigarette aside. "Then I'll radio ComSoPac."

Soon Wallace and Morey and the Wallalua named Makahok were in a fern clump on the perimeter of a Japanese Air Force installation. It was the Imperial 22nd Air Flotilla which, until a week ago, had been in combat flight training at the Bako Naval Station at Kakung, Formosa. This was a formidable force consisting of 23 Mitsubishi Zero fighters, 4 Type 98 land based reconnaissance planes, 16 VB dive bombers and 20 VLB attack bombers.

"I wonder what they're here for?" Morey whispered.

"I'd bet my best teeth," Wallace said, "it's for some kind of mischief against Australia."

This conjecture was correct. The 22nd Flotilla was charged with destruction of Australian-American fleet forces and protection of troop transports carrying the Army Darwin Landing Force, a final deed of Supreme Imperial War Command's First Phase Operations of the invasion of Australia.

Morey and the others crept back to the cove which sheltered the Seahawk. "Start scouting for an inlet with overhanging foliage," Morey said to his men.

It would be prudent to anchor the Seahawk in some other place before he radioed ComSoPac; if the Japanese bombed her in the cove they would be risking incineration-drums of fuel were lashed to the hold and weather decks.

Two harrowing hours later the Seahawk was concealed under interlacing trees which grew from the banks of a fetid jungle river. Then Morey went to the radio and picked up the transmitter. "ComSoPac ... urgent!" he said.

The 22nd Flotilla's monitor, Sgt. Iki Nomura listened incredulously while Morey related the location, number and types of Japanese aircraft. Then this glasses-wearing little Japanese sprinted toward the tent which was the HQ of Col. Ideko Shimobaru, the 22nd's commandant. "Sir ..." he said, bursting into the tent, "an American on this island just radioed his superiors at Darwin. He told them of our location, planes ... everything!"

Shimobaru, who had been lolling on a cot nibbling a mango, leaped up and flung the mango away. He cursed bitterly. This was a maximum disaster—the invasion plan was exposed long before the Japanese were able to launch the invasion! He glared at his aide. "Don't just sit there!" he bellowed. "Tell the pilots to get into the air!" The strategic implications of the radio dialogue were plain to see, he said. Now they had no alternative but to change their tactics from secret operation to open dispersion.

Unfortunately for Col. Shimobaru, the U.S. Navy carrier Cape Esperance was less than 70 miles north of Trangan and already her F4U1 Corsairs-fighters designed to outperform the Japs' vaunted Zeros-were on their way. In addition, a squadron of PBJ-1 patrol bombers (Mitchells) of the 4th Marine Corps Bombing Squadron, based at Lae but which had been flying to Darwin, had changed course and was now speeding toward Trangan with incendiaries, HEs and APs.

Twenty minutes later the 22nd Flotilla had ceased to exist.

(Author's Note: As a consequence of this action the Japanese were forced to postpone indefinitely their planned invasion of northern Australia.)

"I'm not one damn bit sorry," Morey said when night finally came to this exciting but wracking day, "... that we're about to launch the last phase of this 8-ball assignment. Get aboard!" he said, turning to the Wallaluas.

He made Tinuk wait for the final cargo and the day before he loaded this contingent he went with her into the jungle. "This will be the last time," he said.

Tinuk didn't comprehend Morey's words but she understood their significance. She began to love with primitive, vibrant ardor. But this was only a prelude. "Lord..." Morey gasped, though not unhappily.

Two days later the Seahawk sailed into Port Darwin with the last of the Wallaluas.

They were housed in tents in the Woomaburrie, a swampy woods three miles northwest of Darwin. Ten days later Kamekula and his adult sons were scheduled to be flown to New Guinea for the purpose of organizing Wallalua tribesmen in support of the Hollandia invasion.

Kamekula refused to go without the rest of his immense family. "The hell with that mule head!" Col. John D. O'Brien roared after trying for hours to convince Kamekula that ComSoPac could not risk air transportation for the entire family.

The invasion was launched April 22 (1944) with Kamekula still in Australia.

Morey, now a supermarket manager in Texas, served on the destroyer Mayrant during this operation. He spent the remainder of the war as Chief Boatswain on the battleship South Dakota and the cruiser Vicksburg. He never saw his jungle bride again.

THE END

"No, thanks. I don't mix pleasure with pleasure."

MEN...YOU GET ALL TEN
OF THESE TERRIFIC STAG
MOVIE SUBJECTS FOR LESS
THAN THE PRICE OF ONE!

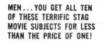
1. Moment of Bliss 2. Savage Delights

3. Fanny Makes Good 4. Beautiful Animal

5. Secret Passions 6. Made In France

7. Lost Inhibitions 8. Boudoir Frantics

9. Forbidden Fruit 10. Coming Out Party

You must be delighted...you must be thrilled...you must agree that these are the most terrific girls you've ever seen in action or your money back!

TEN STAG MOVIE SUBJECTS

all ten only **$2.00**

8mm

GREATEST ADULT MOVIE BARGAIN EVER!

A once-in-a-lifetime opportunity for you to get ten delightfully different, sensationally thrilling stag shows on film FOR LESS THAN THE PRICE OF ONE! Lovely, luscious young beauties go all out to please...ten girls, ten action plots, ten exclusive stag subjects, the kind you've always wanted, the kind only Titan Stag Films gives you!

NOW! DON'T DELAY! SPECIAL LIMITED INTRODUCTORY OFFER FOR NEW CUSTOMERS ONLY!

RUSH $2 CASH, CHECK OR MONEY ORDER (FOR 16mm SEND $4.50)

TO **TITAN STAG FILMS** DEPT. 251
BOX 69856, WEST HOLLYWOOD 69, CALIF.

MOVIE VIEWER SPECIAL
FOR TITAN CUSTOMERS
ONLY **$4.95**

DON'T MISS a thrill, a breath-taking, tantalizing action in Titan Stag Films. New Optic Movie Viewer for 8mm - 50' films gives big, bright, life-like motion pictures for intimate shows; even slow or stop motion. See ad above.

STAG STORIES FOR MEN

ADULTS ONLY

the book nobody dared to print!

COMPLETE—UNABRIDGED—UNCENSORED EDITION MOST DARINGLY INTIMATE BOOK EVER PUBLISHED!

OTHERS PRINT IMITATIONS...WE DARE PRINT THE ORIGINALS! No holds barred! No detail omitted! Scene for scene, act for act, every action is fully described with intimate details word for word and exactly as they were when you passed them around on wallet worn typewritten sheets!

Shocking, racy, old-time favorites such as:

HER ST. BERNARD, THE LOVIN' FAMILY, GASTON & ALPHONSE, THE HOBO & THE SOCIETY GIRL, DEVIL & THE BLONDE!

Plus many *brand new* ones like:

SEVEN DWARFS FOR ADULTS, THE LOVE ATHLETE, WHO MADE THE MAID, HER BIG NIGHT, and many others!

MANY ILLUSTRATED WITH ACTUAL PHOTOS AND DANGEROUS BUT DELIGHTFUL ART!

$2.98 SEND CASH, CHECK OR MONEY ORDER. Sorry, no C.O.D. orders.
GUARANTEED TO PLEASE OR YOUR MONEY BACK!

LIMITED PUBLISHERS GUILD S-41
BOX 69977, Los Angeles 69, California

BEAUTIES FOR THE NAZI ARTIST OF AGONY

By: Jim McDonald
Art by: Unknown
From: **MAN'S BOOK,** April, 1967

No portrait of hell could match the tableux etched by Hitler's foulest fiend

The girls were young, blonde, lovely. Now they stood before the man in the S.S. He watched them through slitted eyes, a little red flush spreading over his smooth shaven cheeks.

He studied their conical breasts which had been thrust outward by the device of having handcuffed their wrists behind their backs. He sighed in contentment. These weren't thick ankled peasants. They had the trim loveliness of the Warsaw upper classes.

"You have been well treated?" he asked, his lips twitching into a thin grimace that was supposed to pass for a smile.

The girls were silent for a moment. They glanced around the room, taking in the bleak barrenness. Boards had been nailed over the windows. The air had the dankness of a tomb about it.

"You have not been molested in any way?" the S.S. captain asked again.

Finally Stephani Wolensky stepped forward. "The chains," she said in a quiet voice, "they chafe my skin."

"I see," Oskar Dirlewanger replied. "And this causes you grave discomfort. Have you any other complaints?"

"We do not understand why we have been arrested. We have done no wrong. We do not understand why we have been spirited to Gostynin."

Dirlewanger grunted. The grunt turned into an obscene scream of a laugh. "Do you hear that, Wepke? They have no idea why they have been brought here."

"Jawohl, Herr Doktor!" his companion answered. "May I suggest that we put an end to their confusion?"

"But of course, my comrade. Let us take them down to the basement. There they will learn to forget their complaints over the slight discomfort of handcuffs."

Dirlewanger pulled a Luger from his holster, waved it at the three girls. His eyes were wild flames, glowing with insanity. His entire face began twitching as he savored the sight of his terrified victims.

"Raus!" he ordered in a voice made shrill by the madness which boiled within him. He moved like a giant cat, measuring his prey. Stephani Wolensky screamed in horror as he encircled her lovely body with his sweating hands, running his fingers over her soft flesh.

His voice became a shrill whisper "You will scream, my pet. You will scream until your throat is a raw bleeding mass. You will scream and your torments will be captured for all to see."

A red haze closed over Stephani's eyes. She felt herself being lifted from her feet. She kicked violently at the man who held her body jackknifed over his shoulder. Her puny efforts brought out a new wave of brutality on his part. She heard screams behind her. Her two companions on the trip from Warsaw were being handled in much the same manner.

But what had come up until now was nothing compared to the sick feeling of revulsion Stephani Wolensky experienced as she saw the chamber for the first time.

The Devil himself could not have devised a more foul place. Her eyes traveled along the hideous engines of torture-the huge wheel standing empty and hungry, waiting to clutch her in the ropes which dangled from it-the thick posts with their heavy gyves ready to encircle her limbs and throat-the abominal rack with its ratchetted gears-the large easel which stood to the side.

Stephani felt the manacles being ripped from her wrists. She barely had time to scream in protest before her back was forced against the wheel, her body arching to its fiendish curve.

Dirlewanger's sweating hands gripped her, dragging her arms upward until they felt as if they must be forced from their sockets. The fiend called Wepke roved his hands under her skirt, slowly trailing his fingers downward to her ankles.

They are binding me to the wheel. They are tying me so that I cannot move a muscle. The ropes hurt. Don't let them do this horrible thing.

In the end she hung before them, her breasts thrust forward, her belly curved, her lovely legs stretched taut. For the moment Dirlewanger tired of Stephani.

He turned his attention to the second blonde girl, supervising Ohlberg as he chained her arms to the post. In like fashion the third girl was fettered.

"A circus!" Dirlewanger mouthed. "A circus of pain!" Spittle flowed freely down his chin. His cheeks were puffed up. He pranced before Stephani, his slitted eyes drinking in every iota of her terror and pain.

He touched the wheel, swinging it slowly. The motion added to Stephani's strain. The ropes dug deeper into her arms and legs.

"Such fine clothing," he cooed. "Such fine clothing when German women must wear ersatz apparel. A dress of silk. Only traitors to the Reich wear silk."

Of all the things that could be done to her, having Oskar Dirlewanger strip her was the most horrible for Stephani. She had but to see his expression to realize he was a sexual psychopath. His touch was like a million foul lizards crawling across her body.

He tore at her dress, tugging and ripping until it lay below the wheel in pitiful tatters. Standing back, he surveyed his handiwork.

A thin film of perspiration covered Stephani's body. She wriggled against the wheel, trying to ease the strain on her extended limbs. She knew how the beast must be enjoying her motions, yet she was powerless to deny him his evil desire.

"The Polish swine wear silk underclothing as well. Perhaps they think they are better than German women," he roared. "We will change all that."

Savagely he reached out. The filmy bra which Stephani wore was wrenched from her virginal breasts. His hands left wild claw marks down her flanks as he shredded her silk panties and hurled them across the room.

Her screams were answered by those of the other two girls. Savagely they were being denuded. The action was a blur of pain and degradation punctuated by the vile mouthings of the Nazi madman.

She heard the sound of a pistol shot. With her eyes closed she prayed that at least one of the girls had been lucky enough to receive a clean death. The pistol-like crack sounded again and a blood curdling scream filled the chamber.

Stephani's eyes flew open. The flip of the whip was still coiled around the naked body of the girl who'd been chained to post. The blonde girl writhed wildly, shifting her weight from one foot to another, clawing at the fetters which held her. A thin red line twisted around her thighs.

Wepke drew the whip over the floor. It slithered over the stone like a giant snake. The lash was at least three feet long and the tip was weighted with a barb.

Dirlewanger now sat at his easel sketching furiously. His eyes were magnetized to the suffering girl. His mouth hung slackly allowing the drool to run down his face unhampered.

Wepke's arm drew back. The whip cracked again, blasting into the girl's hips. She stood stock still for a moment as if stunned by the force of the blow. Then she tugged like a mad woman at her arms, trying to pull them away from her bonds. A trickle of blood ran down her wrist where the skin had been severed.

"Continue, Wepke," Dirlewanger shouted. "I will make up an album for Reichfuhrer Himmler. I will show him how we deal with the Polish filth. He will see my prowess as an artisan. It will be my personal gift to him."

The words became an incoherent babble. Dirlewanger dropped the sketch pad. So transfixed was he by the scene before him that he made no pretense of picking it up.

The whipping went on interminably. When the nude girl finally fainted, they threw a bucket of water over her. It ran down her sagging body turning a sickly pink.

Finally the water could no longer revive her. She was beyond the horrors that Oskar Dirlewanger could perpetrate. Now he turned his attention to Stephani Wolensky. As Wepke watched, he picked up the whip.

Furiously he spun the giant wheel which held Stephani. She moved dizzily, the room blurring before her ves. She felt the blow seconds after it struck. The shock hurled her against the splintery wheel. She had never believed that pain could be so terrible, so all consuming. She heard voices and she saw her tormentors. However nothing was real except the agony which claimed her as its own.

The lash exploded again and again. Her mind was seared with it. She hung on the wheel, constantly spinning, constantly waiting for the next blow. She prayed for death, but they had ways of keeping her alive.

Of all the hideous things that happened in the Dirlewanger torture chamber that night, only the whipping can be mentioned. The only thing that can be said is that the following morning, a detail of concentration camp inmates who had been specially recruited for the purpose entered the basement and cut down three grisly forms who no longer bore any resemblance to human beings.

Stephani Wolensky, a twenty year-old student at the Warsaw Conservatory had died so horribly that no man can imagine her end.

So had Janis Polski and Reba Skorveni.

And what about the murderer? What about Oskar Dirlewanger? In all the annals of barbarity, no man rivals him for sheer bestiality.. He is the summation of all the horrors that were Nazi Germany. More than any other Nazi, he represents the total degradation of a people. He also is the embodiment of the mysterious question of how a nation who gave the world the artisans of literature, music and science could sink into the slime and squalor of depravity which will remain a blot - on all history.

Dirlewanger was not one of the original bully boys of the Munich beer hall riots. He was unlike "Himmler, the former beer salesman or Goering, the narcotics-ridden exWorld War I pilot.

He prided himself on being a man of *kultur*. Records show that he attended several German universities and is said to have won his doctorate in either literature or philosophy. He prided himself on being an amateur artist.

There was another side to Dirlewanger, one that had nothing to do with intellectual pursuits. He was convicted as a sexual criminal and habitual drunk some time before the days of "glory" of Hitler's Reich.

Indeed he was recruited from a prison cell for work with the S.S., main office. There he was trained in the torture methods he was later to spread through Eastern Europe. Dirlewanger was an apt student of sadism. In no time he was given command of the labor camp at Dzika, Poland.

Poland suited Dirlewanger to perfection. For some reason he favored setting up his charnel houses in small villages rather than large cities and Poland was honeycombed with such towns. However his monstrous lieutenants ranged through Warsaw and other areas, selecting victims for what the torturer chose to call his Dirlewanger Circuses.

The typical action followed this pattern. An Einsatzgruppe would seal off an area of a town. All of the inhabitants would be lined up in the streets. Dirlewanger would appear to review the terrified people. Slowly he would walk through the lines of captives who stood trembling, their hands held high over their heads.

All were marked for death, but with Dirlewanger death took different varieties. The young and the beautiful were singled out for very special treatment.

By this time, Dirlewanger had surrounded himself with a group of maniacs who reveled in the screams of lovely young girls. It was for them that women such as Stephani Wolensky were selected and conducted to the waiting torture chambers.

On many occasions the girls were taken to underground cells by twos and threes. There they were chained to the fetid walls, stripped naked and beaten to death with bullwhips.

For variety, Dirlewanger would improvise by injecting the young women with lethal doses of strychnine. No poison known to man can match strychnine for its pain inducing potential.

Their corpses were not even allowed the dignity of burial. Instead their bodies were dismembered and melted down to provide soap for the Nazi overlords.

In any other country, Dirlewanger would have gone to the gibbet for the horrors he perpetrated. But Nazi Germany was like no country the world had seen. The Reich heaped honors on its prime beast. To spread his terror it formed the *Einsatzkommando Dirlewanger* and dredged its own prisons for its most hardened criminals to staff the officers ranks. At the peak of its strength the group reached brigade proportions. It expanded its operations into White Russia, Lithuania and Eastern Poland. Wherever it went it went it walked over torrents of blood and gore squeezed from the populace.

So great were the hideous barbarities it committed that even some Nazis protested to Prinz Albrechtstrasse. The protests were not based on humanitarian considerations, but on the fact that Germany's enemies would be afforded documented accounts of the horrors for propaganda against the Reich.

However Dirlewanger had a 11 direct pipeline to Himmler, Mueller, Streicher and the rest of the top killers and he was given complete license.

Perhaps the ultimate horror of the Nazi regime is that Dirlewanger remained its prototype even after defeat. The tragic fact is that only a relative handful of the butchers who raged through Europe on their rampage of blood lust were caught.

Oskar Dirlewanger was not one of these. After the war he took up a new identity and was swallowed up. Some say he became a turncoat joining Beria's dreaded M.V.D., in Moscow. Others contend that he went to the Middle East to work with certain dictators there.

But as you read this, the chances are that Dirlewanger is standing at this very moment in a stench-ridden underground dungeon watching a chained and beautiful woman being cut to pieces to satisfy his maniacal needs. Drunkard, homosexual, psychopathic sadist, Herr Doktor Oskar Dirlewanger represents all of man's inhumanity from the beginning of time.

THE END

An Amazing Invention—"Magic Art Reproducer"

DRAW ANY PERSON
IN
ONE MINUTE
NO LESSONS! NO TALENT!

Anyone can Draw With This Amazing New Invention— Instantly!

You Can Draw Your Family, Friends, Anything From REAL LIFE— Like An Artist... Even if You CAN'T DRAW A Straight Line!

De Luxe Model Complete for only $1.98

—With extra high power, extra clear and sharp reproducer unit.

A New Hobby Gives You A Brand New Interest!

Yes, anyone from 5 to 80 can draw or sketch or paint anything now ... the very first time you use the "Magic Art Reproducer" like a professional artist—no matter how "hopeless" you think you are! An unlimited variety and amount of drawings can be made. Art is admired and respected by everyone. Most hobbies are expensive, but drawing costs very little, just some inexpensive paper, pencils, crayons, or paint. No costly upkeep, nothing to wear out, no parts to replace. It automatically reproduces anything you want to draw on any sheet of paper. Then easily and quickly follow the lines of the "picture image" with your pencil ... and you have an accurate original drawing that anyone would think an artist had done. No guesswork, no judging sizes and shapes! Reproduces black and white and actual colors for paintings.

Also makes drawing larger or smaller as you wish.

Anyone can use it on any desk, table, board, etc.—indoors or outdoors! Light and compact to be taken wherever you wish. No other lessons or practice or talent needed! You'll be proud to frame your original drawings for a more distinctive touch to your home. Give them to friends as gifts that are "different," appreciated.

Have fun! Be popular! Everyone will ask you to draw them. You'll be in demand! After a short time, you may find you can draw well without the "Magic Art Reproducer" because you have developed a "knack" and feeling artists have—which may lead to a good paying art career.

ALSO EXCELLENT FOR EVERY OTHER TYPE OF DRAWING AND HOBBY!

Create Your Own Design for All Hobbies! Reproduce on anything.

Copy all cartoons, comics.

Outdoor Scenes, landscapes, buildings

Copy photos, portraits of family, friends, etc.

Still life, vases, bowls of fruit, lamps, furniture, all objects.

Copy blueprints, plans.

FREE!
"How to Easily Draw Artists' Models"

This valuable illustrated guide is yours free with order of "Magic Art Reproducer." Packed with pictures showing all the basic poses of artists' models with simple instruction for beginners of art. Includes guidance on anatomy, techniques and figure action.

NORTON PRODUCTS
Dept. **834** 296 Broadway New York 7, N. Y.

SEND NO MONEY!
Free 10-Day Trial!

Just send name and address. Pay postman on delivery $1.98 plus postage. Or send only $1.98 with order and we pay postage. You must be convinced that you can draw anything like an artist, or return merchandise after 10-day trial and your money will be refunded.

FREE 10-DAY TRIAL COUPON

NORTON PRODUCTS, Dept. **834**
296 Broadway, New York 7, N. Y.

Rush my "Magic Art Reproducer" plus FREE illustrated guide "How to Easily Draw Artists' Models." I will pay postman on delivery only $1.98 plus postage. I must be convinced that I can draw anything like an artist, or I can return merchandise after 10-day trial and get my money back.

Name

Address

City & Zone   State

☐ Check here if you wish to save postage by sending only $1.98 with coupon. Same Money Back Guarantee!

HITLER'S BABOON TORTURES IN MABUTI

By: Harris Creeg
Art by: Unknown
From: **MAN'S DARING,** January, 1962

No tortures the Nazis devised were as sadistic as the use of love-starved apes for their experiments on prisoners of war.

(Editor's Note: Dr. Cleeg, a prominent American physiologist, was captured by the Germans during the African campaign. His experiences in the SS concentration camp at Mabuti later prompted him to write the important scientific work "Sexual Experiments of the Nazi Era.")

THE NAZI SCIENTIST, in his black SS uniform, stood grinning by my side. I glanced at his face, a face that had become cruel since we had been students together at the University of Heidelberg before the war. "Don't look at me," he said. "Now it's really getting fascinating. You will see something most interesting."

I followed his command, and shuddered with revulsion. Under any other circumstances I would have turned away, but in the spot I was in I could not afford to betray any weakness. So I gagged down the sour bile that rose in my throat and looked at the horrible scene before me.

Inside the wire cage with the big mandrill baboons were two of the French prisoners who had been brought to the SS camp with me. One was already beyond caring and beyond pain, and it didn't matter what the baboons did to him. But the other was still conscious, his face twisted in a grimace of agony and fear. Grunts of pain escaped from his pale, bloodless lips. Suddenly the grunts changed into a shrill scream, and the eyes popped from his head.

The biggest of the baboons had risen from the lifeless, blood-spattered body of the other man and had pounced on the Frenchman who was still alive. With his big teeth, the big male ape started tearing at the man's belly and groin. Huge spurts of blood gushed from the victim's torn body and splashed over the ape's face as he munched the human flesh. He licked his lips with delight.

"You see Dr. Cleeg," the Nazi doctor said. "It's just as I told you. And I am convinced that I am right about the other thing too. I am absolutely certain that the mandrill, after a diet of human male reproductive tissue, will be capable of pregnating a human female. The result should be very interesting."

I hardly paid attention to his guttaral words. I stared with terror at the dying man in the cage. His screams had stopped. His eyes fluttered and his lips moved feebly. The flow of blood was slowing. Just then one of the smaller baboons jumped on him and finished him off by taking a bite out of his throat.

"Well," said Dr. Hans Brauner, "you have seen for yourself. I give you the chance to work with me."

"And if I say no?"

"In that case," Dr. Brauner smirked, "I shall make use of you anyway. We can always use another healthy male to feed to the baboons."

I shrugged my shoulders, pretending resignation. Perhaps if I managed to gain his confidence I could work up some scheme to escape from the Mabuti torture camp.

MY LANDING IN DR. BRAUNER'S evil hands had been the result of a series of accidental circumstances -the way things work out so often in life, bad things especially. A few days earlier, my commanding officer, back in Casablanca, had told me that the German-speaking member of a Free French commando unit had come down with typhoid fever and that the unit badly needed someone to take his place on an urgent raid 200 miles behind enemy lines. As a former student at a German university, I spoke the language and knew the customs. Would I be willing to volunteer for the mission?

Like a damn fool, I said yes. I was tired of my rear-echelon desk job evaluating scientific intelligence reports. And so, a few hours later, I was on a destroyer steaming toward the Gibraltar Straits and the Mediterranean, and two days later aboard a landing craft chugging toward a deserted beach between Gabes and Tripoli, just about at the border line between Algeria and Libya.

At least we thought it was deserted. It wasn't thanks to an unfortunate second accident. The Fifth SS Sturm Division was holding an exercise in night tactics on the beach the commando unit had picked for its landing and we walked right into the unintended trap. We had no sooner touched land when we were surrounded by laughing Germans who thought they had captured some of their own men playing "enemy." They stopped laughing and started shooting when they discovered their mistake.

We didn't have a chance. Four of the 11 men in the raiding force fell dead in the first burst of submachine gun fire; a heavy grenade blew the landing craft out of the water. The rest of us raised our hands. The jig was up.

For several minutes, after they'd disarmed us, our captors argued whether to kill us on the spot. Just then a command car drew up in the darkness to investigate what the noise had been all about. Two officers climbed out. Somebody shone a harsh light in our faces, blinding us. "French swine," a voice shouted from behind the light, and a fist crashed heavily into my face. I stumbled and fell in the sand.

"This one is not French," another voice said in German. "I think I know the man."

Strong hands gripped my shoulder and yanked me to my feet. The light blinded me again, and I tasted the salty blood that dripped down from my nose.

"*Ja, ja,*" the second voice said. "Ich bin sicher. I am certain. This is an American. He is a spy. He speaks German. We were at the University of Heidelberg together. Wie geht's, Herr Cleeg? How are you, Mr. Cleeg? Not so good, what?"

AND THEN I RECOGNIZED the cynical voice. It belonged to Hans Brauner, the most brilliant student of my class at Heidelberg. Brauner had been an ardent Nazi even then, spouting the superman clap-trap although he should have known better. At the time I had thought that a man with unconventional ideas like his would be a Nazi only for the thrills, and that, in my book, made him a complete swine. I'd told him so on several occasions.

That was the third accident: Brauner, now an SS colonel and commandant of a medical experimentation camp 50 miles inland at Mabuti, had joined the SS division general that night to watch the maneuvers. And he'd recognized me.

He stepped up to me."Well, Mr. Cleeg," he said. "You always thought I was a bastard. Now I shall prove it to you."

I cleared my throat and spat. The ball of phlegm and blood splashed in his face. A split second later, a sharp blow in the back of my neck sent me sprawling in the sand. Somebody kicked at my face with a heavy boot. I gagged on blood and spat out a broken tooth.

"No," Brauner shouted, laughing. "Don't kill him yet. I have much better use for him and the other gentlemen." And then he whispered something I could not understand. The German general started laughing too. "That should be a lot of fun," he said. "I wish I had time to come and watch. But we're going back to the front, day after tomorrow."

"Too bad," Brauner said. "I am sure you would have enjoyed it. Maybe some other time. I have fourteen girls for the experiment and only five baboons, so we shall have fun for quite a while."

The other six prisoners and I were roped together and bundled into the back of a truck. Two guards, their grease guns cocked, glowered at us for the next three hours as the vehicle bounced along the desert road back toward Mabuti—the most notorious camp the Germans maintained in Africa.

I HAD HEARD RUMORS about that camp, and now I would see for myself. My guess was that I wouldn't see for long. It was a place for special punishment and torture operated by the ss for political prisoners, captured Allied agents and commandos. Nobody lasted more than a few days. From the stories I'd heard, it was a place where the Nazis tied prisoners to stakes in the broiling desert sun to see how long men could live without water. I'd also heard that prisoners were used for the preparation of anti-snake venom-exposed to the bites of cobras and mambas and their bodies drained of blood after a tortured death and the blood used in the production of protective serum for the German soldiers. I'd heard about all these things but didn't know what Brauner had been talking about to the general when he had mentioned baboons and girls. I soon found out.

THE NEXT AFTERNOON, BRAUNER -accompanied by a heavily armed guard—came to the hut where I was held in solitary confinement.

"Also," he said. "I hope you feel better, Harris. I want you to appreciate the interesting things we do here. I know you never approved of my ideas, but you must admit that this is unimportant now. You are my prisoner and I can do with you as I wish. Personally, I would prefer not to kill you. You are an excellent physiologist, if I remember correctly, and we are short of scientific personnel."

And then he told me of his pet experiment. The eyes in his cruel face lit up with fanaticism as he talked. "I managed to obtain sixteen beautiful women of different racial strains. Unfortunately, two of them died," he laughed apologetically when my non-coms decided to have some fun with them. They are rather tired of the local Arab women, you know, and I can't blame them. At any rate, fourteer are left and in reasonably good health-healthy enough to conceive children.

"I also managed to obtain five rare mandrill baboons—you know the big ones with the grooved faces and the colored snouts from West Africa. Biologically, as you are well aware, they are the most man-like of the apes. I intend to mate these baboons with the girls and get half-men-half-apes of different human racial background. The results should be very interesting, and perhaps useful. I expect that these creatures will be strong and dumb: perfect slaves. If it works we can kill off all non-Germans—they are not to be trusted and replace them with the new breed."

"You're not only a bastard," I said. "You're crazy. It won't work."

Brauner paled and the sardonic smile left his face. "I warn you," he said. "I don't need you so badly that I will let you insult me indefinitely. I have made my offer of a job to you in good faith ... Anyway, I know your objection. An ape's sperm cannot infructate a human ovum. But you are wrong. I have done it in the laboratory, in a test tube. The baboon I used had been on a diet of human reproductive tissue for several days." His frown turned into a grin again. "There is no shortage of this raw material here. Every day we get new prisoners like yourself."

I stared at him in disbelief. Human reproductive tissue deteriorates immediately after death. What Brauner had said could only mean ...

"You're right," he said, guessing my thoughts, one biologist being able to read the mind of another. "The human subjects must be alive when they are eaten. So far as my guards are concerned, that's part of the fun. Come along. It's almost feeding time."

That was when he took me to the cage where the unspeakable happened, where Brauner's mandrills gnawed at the bodies of my commando comrades of the past week, ripping them apart with their big, sharp apes' teeth, leaving the prisoners to die in the most monstrous torture imaginable man's most severe pain lasting until the last drop of life had drained away.

GUARDS CLEANED OUT THE cage after chasing the baboons off into separate enclosure, their hands tied behind their backs so they could not hurt the apes. Then the runways were opened, and the hungry mandrills, led by the huge baboon, rushed back into the torture cage. The big baboon attacked the first man while he was still on his feet. The man fell with a wild scream, a spout of blood arching from his body.

Another two of the baboons had meanwhile jumped on the other prisoner and were fighting over him. I closed my ears to the inhuman screams.

"The big one is about ready, I think," Brauner said. "Maybe this other one over there too. We'll try them out tomorrow after breakfast.... How would you like to be the breakfast?"

Shivering, I dumbly shook my head.

Lying on the bare floor of the hut that night, I started to make plans. If I was to escape, tomorrow during the torture would be the time. All the sadistic perverts of the SS would be watching the rape of the girls by the baboons, getting their kicks in this erotic new version of peeping-tomism, and they would be paying less attention to me. I just had to convince my old "pal" Brauner that I was interested scientifically and that therefore he could trust me, within limits anyway. I didn't have any worries about what I'd do once I got out of the camp: the African desert is huge and a man is hard to find in it. I could survive in Arab villages until the Germans were thrown out of Africa.

THE NEXT MORNING, THEREFORE, I was wide awake and looking interested but skeptical when Hans Brauner came to fetch me. If I'd looked too enthusiastic, he would have been suspicious. "I still don't believe it," I said.

"You'll see," he said triumphantly. And then he told me what he wanted me to do-it was a simple operation on the girls afterwards, and I hardly paid attention to his instructions because I knew that "afterwards" I'd either be free-or dead.

When we walked outside, the first girl was already trussed for the torture. She was tied spreadeagled to the bamboo poles that held up the barbed wire fence of the camp's perimeter. Two guards, each holding a mandrill on a leash, were standing by, waiting. The baboons were straining at their bonds, trying to get at the girl. They were snuffling and panting, making almost human sounds. The girl's pretty face was contorted in terror. She was dressed only in a slip which had been torn from one shoulder and displayed a lovely breast that seemed to excite the apes as much as it did the ape-like men of the SS complement—about eight of them who stood in a circle to watch the "show."

Brauner gave a signal.

The guard who held the big baboon loosened his grip on the leash and the animal surged forward. It snorted with passion and reached out for the girl. She threw her head back and screamed. The baboon's tough-skinned hands ripped the rest of the slip away. The big beast started squealing with pleasure; the other ape snorted with jealousy. The girl yelled with pain and panic, and the SS men laughed hoarsely and shouted filthy words of advice to the baboon. But the baboon didn't need any advice. He knew what he was doing. The men stopped joking and stared with excited interest. Even the man assigned to guard me stepped forward, forgetting all about me for the moment.

This was my chance. It was now or never. Nobody was looking at me, and they wouldn't look at me for another few minutes. And now the men started cheering and shouting. I could wait no longer. I quickly stepped behind my guard and clamped my arm around his neck, the inside of my elbow squeezing in on his windpipe. He grunted and struggled, but nobody heard or noticed. I increased the pressure. His face turned purple. The submachine gun dropped from his hand and clattered to the ground. Still no one heard. The guard stuck his tongue out between his teeth and it turned purple. The skin on his face turned blue and his eyes rolled up. Just to make sure, I quickly stepped back, releasing my hold at the same time, and with a trick the French commandos had taught me, I dropped him over my raised right knee. A sharp crack told me that I had broken his back.

I reached down and picked up the submachine gun. I could run, duck behind a hut, then vault the fence for a chance at freedom. I'd have a few minutes headway. I had already taken a few steps in the direction where I wanted to escape when I realized that this wasn't right. Almost without wanting to, I turned around and ran toward the SS men. Perhaps there was still time to save the girl.

I pulled back the trigger and fired as I ran. My bullets plowed into the backs of the guards. The heavy slugs bounded them forward as they fell and they lay squirming in the sand. I could tell at a glance that the big baboon had not yet reached his objective but that it would not be much longer. I had to chance it. I had to shoot him before turning my gun on Brauner who was already groping in his holster for his pistol.

I shot the ugly mandrill from the side just as he was about to lower his body on the girl, and raising my submachine gun I shot the other ape and the guard who held him for good measure before I turned the weapon on Brauner. The bolt clicked forward, metal on metal; the magazine was empty.

BRAUNER RAISED HIS PISTOL and fired. The bullet buzzed past my head. I threw my gun at the Nazi scientist. It hit him on the upper chest and the momentum pushed him back against the barbed-wire fence. His jacket caught on the barbs, and as I raced toward him I could see that he had trouble raising and aiming his pistol. I was on him before he could squeeze the trigger again. I kicked him in the groin, then in his face. Full of unspeakable hate, I pushed his head between strands of the barbed wire and then stepped on the strands with both my feet, straddling them on both sides of his ugly face. Blood spurted where the barbs settled in the soft flesh of his neck. His mouth opened and no sound came. Once more he tried to raise his pistol, but by now he was too weak. His arm dropped and twitched.

I took the gun from his lifeless hand. I had no knife and needed the bullets to cut the rope that held the girl. Four more shots rang out and the girl was free. She was only half-conscious but she came along when I pulled her. I picked up a submachine gun from a dead guard as I passed his corpse. With it I pressed down the barbed wire and helped her across. We started running out into the desert.

The girl didn't make it very far, and perhaps it was just as well. We'd only run about fifty feet when some soldiers fired at us from behind. One of the bullets went through her head, and burst out through her face. I kept running. The other girls, at least, were safe from the baboon tortures. The SS might kill them, but without Brauner the ape experiments, at least, would not continue. I found cover behind a dune and raced toward freedom.

THE END

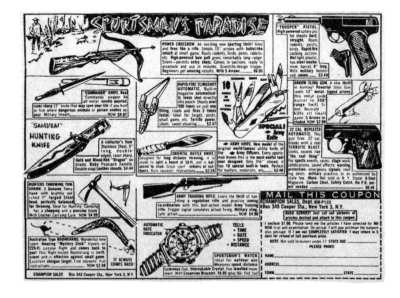

UP TO MY NECK IN LIVE LOBSTERS

By: Josh Lewitt
Art by: Unknown
From: **MAN'S LIFE,** July, 1957

Pincers clacked gouging flesh and bone from me — I screamed and shrieked until I had no mouth — until I was just a red blob covered by green crawling death

FACE down on the bloody slatboard flooring, I regained consciousness, aware of searing pains shooting up my right leg.

Unpegged lobsters-five to fifteen-pounders-were crawling hungrily from a broken live well to the floor, to my body. I lay in a crimson torpor, too weak to defend myself, too hoarse to yell any more. I lay there, being eaten alive, praying for merciful deliverance.

Like swollen slits of flame, both eyes were squeezed so tight I could see the overhead 100-watter as only a vague blur. Head first I'd fallen, the bin shattering under my 200 drunken pounds. Not gloves, not a rubber suit nor boots have given me immunity to those claws. I was lobster feed, and I knew it in every inch of my tortured body.

Pincers clacked over my body like shifting sands, starting from the boots up, crawling on my chest and feeding there. Sobbing, I could only press against the wet, salty bin and in that way shield my face. Yet even in that I failed ...

The night I died was January 1, 1954; more precisely New Year's Eve. To begin with, I wasn't any great shakes at drinking but that night was different. We had a whale of a party at my place, and with good reason. With plenty good reason!

My wife's kid brother, Lucius, had just gotten home from Korea, wounded but alive. Lucius was like my own kid. I'd raised him when both his folks died so having him back meant more than I could possibly put into words. We invited everyone in the neighborhood, and they all brought jugs. I mean it was a celebration!

My business was shipping lobsters to Boston and the New York seafood markets. Frisky lobsters. I'd been in the business for thirty years, and my father before me. The one thing we prided ourselves on was never failing a buyer. Like the postman slogan Neither rain, nor sleet, nor gloom of day shall, etc. In other words, it didn't matter whether the world was coming to an end. The lobsters went through like the mail.

Normally, things were pretty quiet around Kittery at that time. A regular seasonal lull, except for a crazy order now and then. And that was one of 'em. Most lobster fanciers die for a half-pounder, a two-pounder at best. But that order for eight dozen was scheduled for a hell of a banquet, a Moose banquet in Boston, and Mooses the way I got it, wanted everything done on a big scale! Took quite a while to rassle up ninety-six hippy ones, but I had 'em that night and they were scheduled to go out on the noon train.

ONLY thing wrong about the

U night was the fact that they, the lobsters, that is, weren't pegged. A wedge, that is, shoved in the space where their pincers are to keep 'em from tearing each other apart. Normally, the boatmen heft 'em out of their pots and peg 'em as part of their job, but this had been a rush order and I wasn't particular just as long as I could fill it. That's the way things stood when Lucius came home.

Right after midnight the party was going full boil. I was standing with my wife, Betty, under a hunk of mistletoe, planting a big Happy New Year kiss on her pretty mouth when I remembered the shipment. I didn't say anything, though. Just kissed her, made like I was going to the kitchen for another ball and slipped out. Even getting to the kitchen was a rugged sail for me.

"Josh!" the kid grabbed me. "Where you goin'?" He had a ball in his hand and a couple of the local gals under each arm. I knew if I told him he'd insist on coming along so I just grinned stupidly and pointed down.

"The cellar?"

"Yeah!" I shouted. "Got a case of eight-year-old I've been saving for about now"

I had to yell to make myself heard; had to stand on my tiptoes even to see the kid. The blasted kitchen was teeming with people as was every other square inch of my house. The kid bellowed something above the uproar which I didn't get, so I waved and ducked out.

THE lobster bins were around the main house in a square 25-foot cooling shack. I had my work cut for me, to be sure but, once at it, the pegging would buzz right along. I didn't figure anyone would miss me-not with all that cheer flowing like water and I was right. Dead right, practically.

Outside it was cold, and I damned near broke my neck on a patch of ice as I hurried around to the shack. Both feet scudded out from under me, my tail rocketing off the glaze like a guy in a running broadjump. I hit hard, skidding, twisting left and whacking the side of my head against the lobster shack. There I sat, rubbing my dome, laughing drunkenly despite myself.

"Happy New Year jerk!" I slobbered. "Now see if you can stand long enough to peg a few!"

Slowly, gingerly, I pulled myself up, moving to a side of the locker where the oilskins were kept. I didn't use gloves on lobsters normally, but now, suddenly realizing that my reflexes weren't the best in the world, I grabbed the heaviest pair, boots and a jacket and then opened the cooler. Flipping on the overhead light, I saw the net and stood for a moment, staring at crawling green gold. What the hell! I thought dismally. It's better I work it off here than stay upstairs with all that good food and liquor!

THE main pen was a circulating water tank, 12 feet long, aerated, flowing at the far end. Couple of times a week we cleaned the bottom, scraping off the slime, the lobster wastes that congealed in a sickly green film. It was a job that should have been done earlier that week but hadn't been because of the confusion of New Year's and the kid's home-coming. I was used to the stench, though. I took a deep breath, plunged in the scoopnet and dipped under a squirming big one.

The technique, once mastered, was simple enough. Grabbed from behind the head, all they can do is clatter like hell, the big shearlike claws slashing ineptly at air. The peg is driven in head-on, with the carapace held in a position where it can't get traction. The whole thing takes only a couple of seconds and sounds a lot worse than it really is.

Once in a while, sure, someone get's a chunk of meat torn out but those times were damned infrequent. A man either has hands for lobsters or hasn't, in which case he's in some other end of the business. But that night I had hands for nothing.

I stabbed the first squirming crawler I got my net on, pegged him and dumped him in the completed pen. The second, a rangy female with tentacles half a yard long backed furiously from the net, pincers on the ring. I pulled her straight up, knocked her on the tray and grabbed. She scudded through the gloves, and I grabbed again, catching the butt end as she scrambled down the side of the pen.

TRIVE pairs of legs raked over the I gloves and two pincers clamped down. I jerked my hand back, cursing, grabbing again. She cut a neat, deep slice in the finger of my right glove and backed down into the pen. I lunged, my legs suddenly going out from under me and my full 200 pounds crashing into the open trough. I felt myself propelling forward, unable to stop, head on into the tank, and the whole damned tank crashing off its foundation. My head whacked the slatboard flooring like a sack of cement and the overhead light blinked wildly, then faded.

I came to screaming, alive with boiling pains in my left foot, the taste of blood in my throat. My mind was clear enough but not my movements. The simplest thing like getting up off that wet, freezing floor I couldn't manipulate. I heard the loud clacking and scraping of shelled bodies moving over the flooring, and my left boot foot tearing away. It sounded like my wife, ripping an old sheet, but it was my boot and it was hot with a race of blood caused by innumerable pincers having gone through it. I screamed my lungs out, trying to crawl away.

I was face down, the door three yards ahead, the rest of me outstretched in a collapsed pen. I'd landed on my face apparently, for both eyes were swollen almost shut. I tried moving on my belly toward the door but the pains consumed me.

"Christ!" I shrieked. "Somebodysomebody help me!"

All I heard in return were distant sounds of laughter, and the closer, weirder scrapings of lobster shells, incongruous and grotesque in their horror. The sound that was close inundated me. I kept screaming, desperately trying to kick off the tremendous weight on my body. Then I felt them swiveling over my back. Thrashing with my one good leg relieved the weight, but it did nothing as far as getting me away from the pen. In fact, it only made things worse.

MY fingers clawed the bloody slatboards as I inched toward the door, praying I wouldn't lose consciousness. I kept blubbering like a child, staring at my fingers, yet unable to work them. Abruptly, the weight on my left leg shifted to the center of my back and the pincers began digging through rubber there. God was merciful. I passed out again. For too long.

When I regained consciousness, my right leg from the kneecap was numb, and my left to the hip felt as though I'd stuck it in a cauldron of hot oil. I rolled over, blinking at the vague overhead light, the bodies of lobsters cold and squirming, crushed beneath me as I shifted my weight. I saw it then my left leg or what was left of it. Just the black, jagged upper part of the boot. I saw my shinbone protruding grey through the pool of gore, and the boot foot being dragged away.

I collapsed, lying there, too hoarse to shout any more, too weak to edge to the door. The light kept fading and the spreading numbness brought the stench of my own weird death into focus. I began to gag, then vomited, trying to shield my face as the race of thick green bodies poured over me. I didn't even do a good job of that.

Three mornings later when they brought me around, I found myself wishing I were dead. My right ear, my left foot and God knows how many slices of meat where the rubber coat had opened! Not shock treatment, not even the best therapeutists and chaplains could tell me life was worth living. I'd been eaten by lobsters, a twist, to be sure but eaten. It's three years later and I've got a hearing aid and an artificial limb. That gets me around. I'm in a different business. The only thing it doesn't do is keep my mind from going back to the vivid horror of a certain New Year's Eve.

I got out under my own power, they told me. When the party broke up somebody remembered the host.

I was half in the cooler, and half out, and the part that was in was chewed away, left foot first. I never did find out how the Moose banquet turned out.

THE END

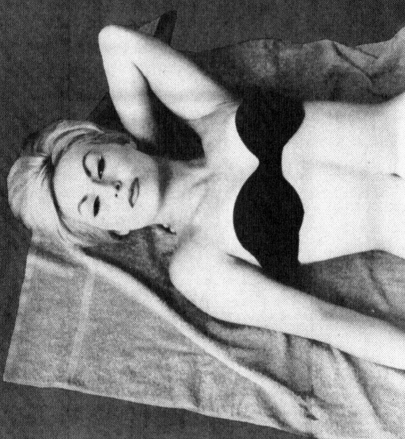

We're sure in for plenty of clear sailing ahead because honey blonde model-actress CLAIRE SHAW is at the helm.

When her day is through, the California-bred, Texas-born cutie loves to sit in her suite and dream about boats.

BORROW BY MAIL!
ONLY $54.00 A MONTH REPAYS $1215

Borrow $111 to $1215 entirely by mail! Pay all your bills with a confidential loan from Postal; only one small monthly payment instead of many. Over 55 years of dependable service to people throughout the U.S.A. State-licensed—your assurance of fair rates and supervised reliability. Fast, Airmail Service. Try Us!

POSTAL FINANCE CO., Dept. 42A
200 Keeline Building
Omaha, Nebraska 68102

SELECT LOAN HERE

Cash You Received!	30 Monthly Payments
$111.	$ 5.00
$315.	15.00
$510.	24.00
$1000.	45.00
$1215.	54.00

D. J. Levitt, President
POSTAL FINANCE CO., Dept. 42A
200 Keeline Building
Omaha, Nebraska 68102
Rush FREE complete Loan Papers.

AMOUNT NEEDED $_____

Name_____Age_____
Address_____
City_____State_____Zip Code____

POEMS WANTED
To Be Set To Music
Send one or more of your best poems today for FREE EXAMINATION. Any Subject. Immediate Consideration.
Phonograph Records Made
CROWN MUSIC CO., 49 W. 32 St., Studio B02 New York 1

BEER 6c Quart / WINE 25c Gallon

Easy to follow instructions for delicious home-brew. Amazing punch & vigor. cheap too. Send $1.00 to
ARTEK FORMULA Dept. 2663
6311 Yucca St., Hollywood 28, California

HYPNOTIZE

Hypnotism revealed! Learn this amazing, fascinating science. Taught by the world's leading professional hypnotist. Write today for FREE, illustrated details:

MEL POWERS — Dept. 2663
8721 Sunset Blvd., Hollywood, California 90069

HEAR WHISPERED SECRET CONVERSATIONS
...thru SOLID WALLS

NOW — with ordinary materials you can easily make a Super Directional Mike that amplifies sound 1,000 times. YES, YOU CAN ACTUALLY HEAR CONVERSATIONS THRU WALLS A BLOCK AWAY. Used by intelligence agents. So simple to make, that you will be using your Super Directional Mike 15 minutes after you obtain the ordinary store materials. Easy instructions.

Only $1.00 from: **SOUND WAVE, Dept. 2663**
862 No. Fairfax Ave. Los Angeles 46, Calif.

53 VARGAS GIRLS
Playing Cards In Full Color!
Your private collection by Playboy's favorite creator of luscious lovelies. No two alike. Finest quality, plastic coated. Adds fun, zest to every card game.
52 AMERICAN BEAUTIES (shown above) All-time favorite Calendar Girls posed as you like 'em! Each deck just $2 ppd. or both decks in Gift-Pak, $3.95. Vargas-Vanities, P.O. Box 622-F, St. Louis 88, Mo.

PELLET FIRING "45" CAL. AUTOMATIC
Magazine Loading Ammunition Clip - Has Automatic Slide Action — Over 15 Moving Parts

$1.00

Fires 8 Rounds
An automatic full size model of a high powered "45" caliber automatic pistol that looks and feels just like the real thing and contains over 15 moving parts. Loads 8 complete rounds in the magazine clip which snaps into the hard butt just like an army "45". Then fires 8 bullet-like pellets as fast as you can pull the trigger. You've got to see the automatic slide action and feel the power to believe it! Great for shooting fun. This is the most authentic model gun we've ever seen.

Learn the Working Mechanism of a "45"
This accurate model of a high-powered, "45" comes to you disassembled with all the working parts of a "45". It assembles in a jiffy and full instructions are included so that in no time at all, you'll learn working parts of an automatic. Comes with instructions, full supply of pellets and man-sized silhouette target.

10 Day Free Trial
Try it for 10 days free. If you are not 100% delighted simply return after 10 days for prompt refund of full purchase price. Don't delay! Order now! Simply send $1 plus 25c shipping charge to:

HONOR HOUSE PRODUCTS Dept. PA-76
Lynbrook, N. Y.

SEWS LEATHER
AND TOUGH TEXTILES LIKE A MACHINE

With **SPEEDY STITCHER** Automatic Sewing Awl, anyone can quickly and skillfully sew or repair anything made of LEATHER, CANVAS, NYLON, PLASTIC, or other heavy materials. Sews firm, even lock-stitches like a machine. Gets into hard-to-reach places. Specially made for heavy duty sewing on LUGGAGE, FOOTWEAR, RUGS, AWNINGS, SAILS, SADDLERY, UPHOLSTERY, OVER-ALLS, AUTO-TOPS, SPORTS GEAR, and other tough sewing jobs. Here's the handiest tool you'll ever own. Will save you many times its small cost. Comes ready for instant use, complete with bobbin of waxed thread and 3 different types of diamond-pointed needles. Easy-to-follow directions will make you an expert in minutes. Extra needles and waxed-thread always available. Save money, send $1.98 for postpaid delivery. If C.O.D. $1.98 plus postage. MONEY BACK GUARANTEE.

ONLY $1.98

SPORTSMAN'S POST
366 Madison Ave., Dept. A-143 New York 17

AMAZING NEW AIR-CUSHION SUPPORT FOR RUPTURE

Comfortaire Truss with adjustable pressure inflated pad shaped for securest most comfortable rupture support. 30-day free trial. Money-back satisfaction guarantee. Write now for free literature.

COMFORT APPLIANCE CO.
403-409 University Street
Healdsburg 12, California

LOVE IN A SUITCASE
Confessions of a Convention Queen

By: Marie Nolan
Art by: Unknown
From: **MAN'S LIFE,** July, 1957

When the boys look for something extra special in the way of room service, I arrive. Believe me, the tired executive won't be tired long.

I felt the big goon's ham-like paw grind into my shoulder with a bone crushing grip. Even though the paying customers were paying close attention to the aquacade going on in the pool, I felt like every eye in the place was on me.

"Let's go, Suzie. No-fuss, no nonsense. Let's just march on out whistling Dixie," the goon sneered.

Slowly I got to my feet. I knew better than to create a scene. That's the mark of the real amateur. The "who me?" stuff is as phony as a three dollar bill. When you've gone into my type of work, you know there are certain risks involved.

So I pursed my lips and let the first halting strains of Dixie whistle through them. The big house man acting like a prize dog catcher hustled me through the narrow aisles between tables. In a matter of seconds we were turning into a narrow door marked Security.

The hotel's house detective sat ensconced behind his formica topped desk. We nodded to each other and he offered me a cigarette.

"What's the beef, Harry?" I asked.

"Got a complaint, Suzie. Guy in 1439, was hustled and rolled. Claims he was given a mickey."

"Go on, that's a lousy rap and you know it."

Harry grinned broadly. "Of course it is.. That isn't your style. But I had to make a show of doing something. The guy doesn't want to press charges. Just wants the satisfaction of seeing somebody hauled in. He'll go home happy."

"Okay so you made your play. Can I go now?"

"Sure, why not? Only keep away from here until the grocers pack up and go home. It's only another couple of days. Besides, there are plenty of other hotels to work on the Beach."

"I'll be seeing you, Harry," I grinned, as I ground my cigarette out in the onyx ashtray.

"You bet. Let me know when you're handing out some free samples. I might be interested."

"For you any time," I laughed back over my shoulder. Both Harry and I knew we were kidding each other. The hired help doesn't mix socially with the professional convention girl. It doesn't make for good business.

I knew it wouldn't be a week before Harry would be back to me with a hot referral.

The truth of the matter is that convention call girls couldn't last a minute without the cooperation of hotel staff as well as convention managers. Practically every city in the country is starved for convention business. When the boys get away from home, they spend money on everything from a four bit cigar to a couple of thousand at the local track.

The hotels know this. The convention bureaus know this. So why ruin the touring John's fun by keeping girls like me away from him.

OF course there's an unwritten law that concerns fleecing or blackmail. No resort area will stand still and allow this type of reputation to get around. That's why Harry had picked a time when all the grocers were congregated around the pool watching the water ballet to put the bite on me.

Every one of the pot bellied boys could breathe a little easier believing his indiscretions were being protected.

But melodrama like that is the exception rather than the rule. For the most part, I'm free to circulate around any hotel you might care to name. No matter how large the crowd which clamors around the reservation desk, I can always get a house room just by snapping my fingers. What I have to offer is as important to a successful convention as the palm trees and speech making.

I've learned a lot about this business. First of all I know the hot towns and those which are dead as doornails. I've learned these facts the hard way.

For example despite whatever you might have heard to the contrary, New York for all its bright lights is really a hick town. It's priggish and stuffy and puts a premium on false morality. The type of conclave it books is not for me.

Most New York conventions are made up of large groups of flunkies.

Take the retailers. They send their buyers and merchandise men once a year. They attend day and night meetings. They are expected to render detailed reports to the brass when they get back home. If at the end of one of these round-the-clock sessions, they're able to make it down to the cigar counter in the lobby for the morning papers, they're doing very well.

Now down here in Miami, we have an entirely different situation. Most associations and companies schedule meetings here in the hopes of currying favor with their membership, or giving employees a well earned rest from home office and little woman. The boys are here to play.

All I have to do is buy a copy of the local newspaper and take my pick of hotels. If there's a union executive board anywhere around I'll give that a top priority. Those boys have unlimited funds at their disposal. They'll throw it around with no questions asked.

Of course I've gotten into some pretty rough brawls where the so-called labor leadership was made up of nothing but yeggs. I remember one night when I was called to the presidential suite of a plush hotel. Three hairy goons were already stripped down to their shorts and undershirts.

"Come on girlie, get with it," they ordered. "We've been waiting a long time."

"Are you crazy? There are plenty of working girls in town. I'm not taking on all three of you," I shouted.

"Hey, a hellcat," one of the beefy characters chortled. "I like a dame with spirit. But I guess this one needs some cooling off."

I sputtered like a wet hen as he picked me up and carried me still fully clothed into the shower. The bastards stood around holding their sides laughing as I felt the full force of the needle spray splashing ice cold through my clothes.

The action with the goons took long enough for my dress to dry thoroughly. The guys were rough and primitive. But they were good sports. Before I left, they pushed five $100 bills into my hands.

FOR the most part I steer away from college fraternity clambakes. I'm not going to waste my time nursing some sophomore from State U who hasn't learned how to hold his whiskey. Besides, the college boys are mostly on an allowance from the old man. They try to make five dollars sound like the national debt.

Of course the best deals of all are the sales conventions. There you get your money both ways. This is a relatively new wrinkle. Here's the way it works. A large manufacturer—say of television sets or housewares invites its dealers to attend a sales meeting.

The dealers show up. In some cases it's in a large hotel. In others it's a chartered section of a cruise ship. If the boys ever draw a breath sober enough to study the sales charts or putter around with the gadgets on the new model, it's a minor miracle.

Now before the event takes place, the manufacturer sends advance men into the city. They scour the bars picking up bits of information about the availability of working girls. They interview us and pay us a retainer. These public relations and advertising tyros know everything there is to know about psychology. They understand that if a dealer meets a girl and she appears to be an amateur, he's going to be all the happier. So we're instructed to fight just a little bit, before we pull down our panties.

The retailer gets an evening's entertainment so he's satisfied. Me, I get my money in advance so I don't have to worry about the client's credit rating. The manufacturer's salesman has something to talk to the mark about the next time he visits him in his home store. It's all very nice and it adds up to beautiful profits for the manufacturer.

The local people work all kinds of crazy deals too. I know one boat dealer who offers any publicity man a fully stocked yacht for demonstration purposes for as long as a week at a time. He charges a straight fee for boat and girls.

I've worked with this boat dealer on many occasions. For the most part the passion cruises have been a lot of fun. You get a bunch of high powered executives out to sea, pull the corks out of the best Kentucky Bourbon and anything goes.

It's always a show watching the fifty year-old Johns trying to cavort like college kids. It's all you can do to keep from laughing at the way they try to suck their bellies in before the go over the side of the boat in those nude moonlight swimming parties.

But tact is my stock in trade. He may be 250 pounds of solid blubber, but when I'm in his company he's Tarzan on a spree.

Of course there's always some danger involved in the cruise routine. If things get ugly, there's a long swim home. So you just have to stay aboard and hope for the best.

I remember one night when we'd sailed aboard an 83 footer. There were about ten girls and just about that number of men. Some advertising veep had concocted the idea.

As the evening went on, a guy by the name of Bill Watson began to get uglier and uglier. His language was foul and abusive. As luck would have it I'd been paired off with him. I tried to shame him into behaving. "Look, Bill. You're a big time tycoon. You don't want to sound like a truck driver," I cajoled.

"I'm paying for this damned trip and I'll sound any way I please," he spat back.

I caught the advertising veep's eye and shook my head helplessly. He immediately detached himself from the blonde who had been sprawled across his lap. He made his way to me very shakily.

"Don't start any trouble," he said in a nasty tone. "It could mean my job."

"I'm not starting anything. But if that big creep doesn't keep his fat mouth shut, I might finish a thing or two," I warned.

The veep put a consoling arm around my bare shoulder. "Honey, I know the guy's an unmitigated bastard, but he's very important to me. Pays me fifty thousand a year. I can't antagonize him."

"That's your hard luck, junior. I don't know him from Adam."

"Baby, you stick with him no matter what. Just for tonight. And I'll personally pay you a bonus of a thousand. Is it a deal?"

I stuck out my hand and grinned. "It's a deal, friend." For a thousand dollars, I thought I could put up with anything.

Brother how wrong I was. When the big hyena got me down to his cabin, he started working me over with a leather belt. He cut every stitch of clothing from my burning hide. The more I cursed and cried, the more of a charge he got out of it. I realized he was an incurable sadist.

When he finally sobered up towards morning the tycoon became extremely remorseful. He launched into a tirade about how he'd always been dominated by shrewish women—first his mother and sisters and now his sharp tongued wife. The only release he could get was by finding some working girl and beating the hell out of her. Every blow she took was, in reality, aimed at the women who had shared his life.

Would you believe it, I felt sorry for the weirdo. All in all it wasn't too bad a deal. He gave me fifteen hundred.

There have been a couple of odd ball experiences like that. But for the most part it's routine. I've had a few years of it now, and I know I'm beginning to grow a little old for the convention stuff. The boys will be looking around for younger faces soon.

But when the day comes that I have to get out, I won't have much to worry | about. I've earned big money and I've listened to the best financial brains in the country. From the latest reading of the stock market ticker, I've made some pretty shrewd investments. Who knows, | I may even move north again.

THE END

NICKI GIBSON & THE GIRLS

Meet some of the ladies of **MAN'S BOOK**, **MAN'S DARING**, **MAN'S PERIL**, and **MAN'S STORY**...

Gibson may be her name, but no "Gibson Girl" she. Prim U and proper and prudish she isn't. Pert and perky and pulchritudinous she is. She's Irish, and the curvy Colleen is rightfully proud as punch that she hails from Eire.

If the Emerald Isle produced not a single poet or playwright, the world would still be eternally beholden to it for the glorious girls that Ireland grows. As numerous as shamrocks they are—but beauties like Nicki Gibson come as scarce as the four-leafed ones.

Valerie Allen

Valerie Allen is an Iowa-born beauty pageant winner who made the move West to Hollywood.

Bonnie Bentley

When she's not on a TV assignment, our gal is really up in the air— in her own, twin-engine Apache. Any volunteers for co-pilot, fellows?

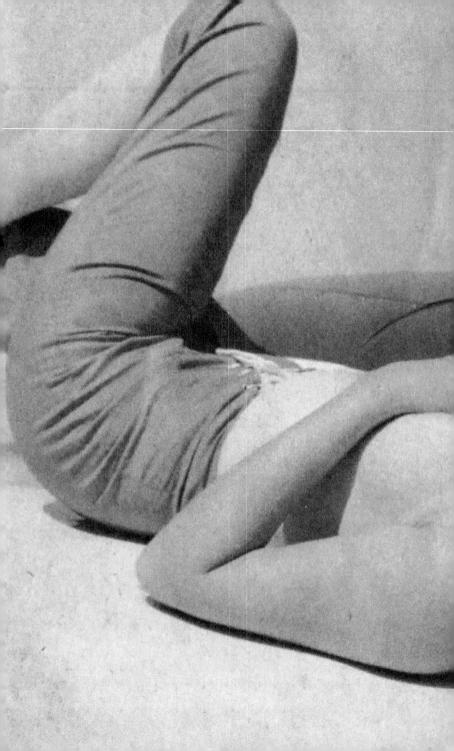

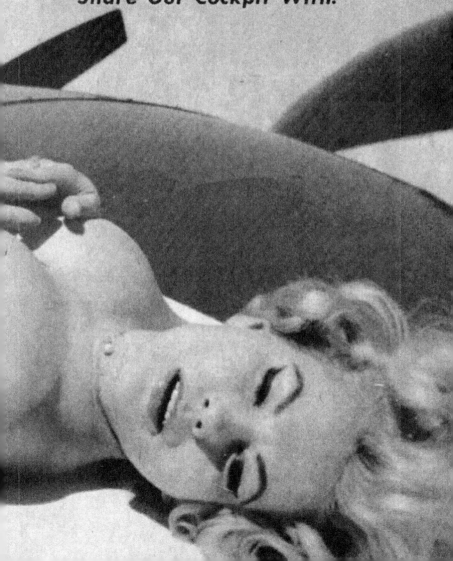

Bonnie is 5'6", weighs 112 and measures in at 36-23-36. All of which earns her the title of Girl We'd Most like To Share Our Cockpit With.

CURIOUS?

I have some intimate, uncensored photos from my personal collection that may be of interest to you. Not the ordinary kind. 12 4x5's only $1.00

LARA 1 Orchard St. Dept. 74 N.Y. 2, N.Y.

PHONOGRAPHIC FILMS

NOW available due to latest decision. SEE and HEAR these two in their fantasy of extasy. For 8mm copy and info. send $1.

SARRY INTERN'L · 6311 YUCCA
HOLLYWOOD 28, CALIF.
Dept. 673

LIBERAL WEST COAST COUPLE

Interested in home made movies, will SELL or SWAP films of unusual indoor activity. Send $5 for movie or $1 for Polaroid photos to T&L. P.O. Box 27041, Hollywood, California 90027 Dept.673

MORE FUN...

$1.00 Postpaid

A parody of **MARITAL LOVE** 12 MODERN POSITIONS

20th Century woman demands more! Here for the first time, fully illustrated, the way modern man keeps her happy. Send a copy to all your friends. Shipped in a plain wrapper.

ADE BOOK BOX 11043 DEPT. LRM-10
AMES AVE. STA. — OMAHA, NEBR. 68111

You Fellow Sportsmen
NO MATTER WHAT YOUR AGE
I'll Show YOU FREE by my quick SECRETS

How to GAIN or LOSE UP TO 60 LBS

HOW TO BUILD THE **TOUGHEST HE-MAN BODY**
In 10 Minutes a day in 30 Days!

'YES, I'LL GIVE YOU GIANT STRENGTH to buck the toughest trail to land the fightingest fish! IN DOUBLE-QUICK TIME YOU'LL LAND A RIP-ROARING BODY, Flat strap stomach muscles, Iron arms and legs, Herculean shoulders and back. I've done it for THOUSANDS like YOU, I'll do it for YOU!

AMERICAN BODY BUILDING CLUB,
Dept RMG-7 GREAT NECK, N.Y.

Send me **FREE!** All these 5 famous PICTURE-PACKED Test Courses (formerly $5. each) to make me A SUPERMAN
I enclose 25c for postage

NAME_____
(Please Print Clearly)
ADDRESS_____ AGE___
CITY_____ ZONE___ STATE___

Adults! See the "VIBRATOR"

A thrilling experience! (Not a pin-up movie.) Send fifty cents for brochure and free sample still photo. FEATHERS, 863 N. Virgil Ave., Los Angeles, Calif. 90029. Dept. RM7

TURN ON MAKE THE Scene

WITH OUR NEW HOT HIPPY STAG FILMS
NO KID STUFF YOU MUST BE OVER 21
FILMED INDOORS BY 'WAY-OUT' COLLEGE STUDENTS

SEND $1 GET $2 BACK
1st TIME AVAILABLE
CRASH-PAD FOTOS, FILMS and SLIDES

★ 12 pg. fully illustrated catalog
★ $2.00 GIFT Certificate
★ Sample film strip of 12 different nudes.

Send $1 and we'll apply $2 to your first purchase
DARLEENE SALES Dept. N 1
Box 147 RESEDA, CALIFORNIA 91335

FREE FACTS on how to become
GOVERNMENT HUNTER
Game Warden, Forester
Positions That Require Less Formal Education

Don't be chained to desk, machine or store counter. Prepare now in spare time for exciting career in Conservation. Many Forestry & Wildlife men hunt mountain lions, parachute from planes to help marooned animals or save injured campers. Plan to live outdoor life you love. Sleep under pines. Catch breakfast from icy streams. Feel and look like a million.

OPPORTUNITIES IN YOUR STATE?
We show you how to seek out job openings in your state and others coast to coast. Good pay, low living costs, no layoffs. Age 17-45, sometimes older on private game farms and hunt clubs. Live a life of thrills and adventure.
FREE! 20-page Conservation Career BOOK, plus aptitude QUIZ and Subscription to Conservation MAGAZINE. State your age. Rush name today! Accredited member NHSC

NORTH AMERICAN SCHOOL OF CONSERVATION
4 East 46th St., Dept. RMG-7 New York, N.Y. 10017

BUY U.S. SAVINGS BONDS

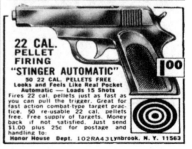

22 CAL. PELLET FIRING
"STINGER AUTOMATIC" $100

50 22 CAL. PELLETS FREE
Looks and Feels Like Real Pocket Automatic — Loads 15 Shots
Fires 22 cal. pellets just as fast as you can pull the trigger. Great for fast action combat-type target practice. 50 re-usable 22 cal. pellets free. Free supply of targets. Money back if not satisfied. Just send $1.00 plus 25c for postage and handling to:
Honor House Dept. 102RA43 Lynbrook, N.Y. 11563

THE TATTOO GANG'S VICIOUS FIRE TORTURE OF THE SOCIETY DEBS

By: Kenneth Seward
Art by: Unknown
From: **MAN'S PERIL,** January, 1965

He swung the branding iron through the air...and with the sibilant hiss of burning flesh, it plunged into the soft skin of the young blonde's thigh...

WITH EACH frantic beat of her heart, the ugly, red welts on the young blonde's milk white fleshi hurt more and more. Hoping against hope, she tugged at the coarse, hemp rope that bound her wrists behind her back. It was futile. The harder she tried to release herself, the more tightly the rope bound her-the more painfully it bit into the soft, tender skin of her arms.

Suddenly, she heard a shrill scream-loud and high pitched, rising eerily above the roar of the surf. She knew what it meant: Another of her playgirl friends had just been marked for life by the branding iron of the tattoo terrorists.

The blonde squeezed her eyes shut, as if that could blot out the thought of what she knew was taking place a few feet away from her. Yet, she still could picture the girl. And hear her.

Now, a strange and pungent odor assailed her nostrils: The odor of burning human flesh!

"Ahora! Aquella!"

The harsh, nasal basso barked the words authoritatively. The blonde had only one year of high school Spanish, but she knew what he meant. "Now! That one over there!"

And she was the one he was talking about!

A pair of coarse, masculine hands roughly gripped each of her arms. Squinting open her eyes, saw that she was being lifted from the sand by Pancho and Pajaro-two of the members of the gang of tattooed maniacs she and her girl friends had first flirted with, then been captured by more than a week ago on a desolate beach in Puerto Rico.

It had seemed so innocent then, and the men in the gang had seemed so quaint, so interesting, what with their sinewy, sun-bronzed bodies and their gleaming, swarthy smiles and the obscene pictures tattooed all over their skin. Little did she or any of her girl friends realize at the time that they were flirting with danger and courting disaster at the hands of Las Peliculas, one of the most demented and feared groups of terrorists ever to prowl the wilds of Central America.

Despacio!" barked the basso. 'Hace mucho tiempo!

"Slowly," it meant. "There's plenty of time."

Clearly, he was getting immense enjoyment out of watching her struggle. And why not? Wasn't she the most beautiful of the six girls? His very special favorite? And wasn't that the reason he had saved her for last?

The blonde looked at him. El Diablo, he called himself. The Devil. And that's exactly what he looked like, standing next to the huge, flat stone on the beach, the flickering yellow light from the fire accentuating his diabolically-angular face and casting weird shadows across his gleaming, bare chest.

His white teeth gleamed in a sadistic smile as Pancho and Pajaro brought the blonde before him. He looked momentarily at the glowing brazier alongside him, where the long branding irons were heating among the red-hot coals.

"Please, Diablo, don't brand me," the blonde begged, dropping to her knees in front of him, "I'll do anything you say. I'll even do all those things you said you wanted me to do last night. Anything, Diablo, do you understand me? Anything!"

Diablo only smiled-almost ruefully, as if to say that he regretted that her request was beyond his power to grant.

"Oh, please," she went on, whimpering. Please don't brand me. I've promised you I'll do anything. What more can I say?"

His smile broadened. He watched the hot, fearful tears stream down her blood-drained cheeks. He watched her bruised and welt-covered body trembling in the crisp, Caribbean breeze. And, his black eyes gleaming, he gestured with his head to Pancho and Pajaro.

BRANDING IRONS The two men forced her pliant body over the stone, then pried her 'long, slender legs wide apart. A third man seized one of the hell-hot irons from the brazier and handed it to El Diablo. A ritual cry of delight burst from the crowd of tattooed Latins gathered around the rock. His smile broader and fiercer than ever, El Diablo brandished the glowing iron above his head. Then he stepped forward toward the helpless, supine, spread-eagled young blonde.

Suddenly, from somewhere in the sky out over the ocean, came an ominous and mysterious roar. Surprised, the members of the tattoo gang turned and looked in the direction of the sound.

Unbelievably, a helicopter was descending upon the scene. In it were a pair of burly, rough-faced men in American attire-both of whom held cradled in their arms .30 calibre submachine guns!

"Venga!" shouted Pajaro, releasing his grip on the girl. "Vamonos!" ("Come on! Let's get out of here!")

"No! barked El Diablo. "Fuego!" ("No! Fire at them!")

Obediently, the diabolical Latin's tattooed cohorts whipped out their pistols and began firing at the glassdomed helicopter. They received, in reply, a barrage of fire from one of the .30 calibre submachine guns. And the helicopter moved in closer to the beach.

El Diablo threw a hasty glance over his shoulder at the copter. Then, before taking cover and entering the gun battle, he did the one thing he had been waiting to do since he got out of the blonde's bed that morning -he swung the glowing branding iron through the air and, with a sibilant hiss of burning flesh, plunged it into the soft, tender skin on the inside of her thigh.

Her anguished scream went unheard in the echo of the second round of bullets coming from the copter.

"Keep your fire over their heads," said private detective and former-FBI agent Nat Price to his partner, Paul Saunders, as the aircraft moved in for a landing on the beach. "We don't want to hit any of the girls by accident."

Saunders pulled back on the trigger and watched another volley of shots tear into the sand, a good distance behind the tattoo gang and their captives. A pistol shot from one of the tattooed desperados whizzed by just inches above the copter's glass dome.

"Roger," said Saunders; "only those bastards are coming mighty damned close ..."

Two weeks earlier, when the six girls departed unannounced for a Caribbean vacation, they had no idea who in the world Nat Price and Paul Saunders were–let alone that, before long, their very lives would depend on them.

The girls, a group of pampered and undisciplined young debutantes from wealthy families, decided that another winter at Palm Beach, Florida, would be just too-too-terribly boring to bear. They thought of journeying downstate to Miami Beach or Fort Lauderdale, but dismissed both spots as gauche. Then, their judgement as bad as their French, they settled on a plan to explore the Caribbean.

There was only one hitch. Even their moneyed moms and dads, long victims of the Dr. Spock nonsense that says, "Let the kids have their way," wouldn't consent to an unchaperoned Caribbean jaunt. Accordingly, the six of them told their parents that they'd be staying in Miami Beach; but, as soon as they got out of one plane at Miami International Airport, they got aboard another one-destination: Puerto Rico.

Loaded with that good green stuff that makes American babes welcome everywhere, even if they don't happen to be beautiful-which these six happened to be!—they found themselves getting the red carpet treatment all over San Juan. In the interests of not creating any suspicions, they split up into three groups of two and checked into different hotels under assumed names—two into the Condado Beach Hotel, two into La Ponce and two into the Caribe Hilton. Moreover, to cover their tracks, they had pre-arranged for a girl friend of theirs in Miami Beach to send postcards (which they had filled out in advance) to their parents, one every two days for a month.

For a while, San Juan had everything the girls needed to slake their jaded thirsts for kicks. Two of the group, who happened to like women as well as men, swung not only with each other but with several of the low-priced beauties who peddle their assets to anyone, male or female, that has a spare $10 bill. The other four, heterosexually oriented, swung with beach boys and Puerto Rican entertainers. Between bouts in the bedroom, they whiled away their time in the gambling casinos or in the sleazy, rock-and-roll dives that abound in San Juan Antiguo.

After several days, however, even this fast pace began to lose its charm. Bored again, they decided to set out for the interior of the island and explore the areas where tourists normally don't set foot.

While the girls were making their way inland in a rented automobile, a 45-foot cabin cruiser was sailing out of Guatemala Harbor. In the captain's chair on the bridge was the swarthy Latin who called himself El Diablo. Elsewhere on the vessel were a dozen or so men, all in their mid-twenties to early-thirties, who called themselves Las Peliculas ("The Pictures").

TERROR OF THE BEACHES

For more than five years now, El Diablo and Las Peliculas had been terrorizing the beaches of the Central America and Caribbean countries. The group, known by the manner in which each of its members was almost completely covered with tattoos, specialized in kidnapping teen age girls and young women, forcing them to submit to every imaginable sexual indignity and then branding them with the same type of branding irons that are used for cattle!

Usually, the group would bring its branded victims to Brazil and sell them to white slave enterpreneurs. Sometimes, when the girls were so horribly burned and maimed from the Peliculas ritual that the white slavers would not buy them, they were murdered and their bodies were thrown into the sea.

The kidnapping and branding practices of the group and the subsequent sale of the victims were not primarily part of the commercial enterprise. Rather, it was the way the demented Latin gang got its thrills. Most of the members of Las Peliculas were wealthy exiles who had managed to take enough money with them to last the rest of their lives. El Diablo, himself, was said to have been a prosperous whoremaster in Battisfa's Cuba before the 1958 revolution. Some of the others were reportedly fellow Cubans, while still others were said to be from Panama, Nicaragua, Guatemala or the countries of South America.

Prior to departing from Guatemala, the group had just experienced a close brush with the law. They had kidnapped three young girls from a village near Guatemala City and had brought them to a beach for the branding ceremony. Sharp-eyed village policemen were on their trail, however, and, before the ceremony could take place, Las Peliculas were forced to flee the country.

Now, their appetites whetted by this near miss, the group headed for Puerto Rico. Ordinarily they avoided operating in territories that were the possessions of the United States or Britain, because law enforcement here is considerably more strict than in the southern regions. But, since things seemed too "hot" at the Guatemalan home base and in other Central American countries, they decided on one Puerto Rico strike to pass the time while they were waiting for things to "cool off."

As the cabin cruiser approached the Puerto Rican coast, El Diablo gave last-minute instructions to his confederates.

The boat, he explained, would anchor off the southeastern tip of the island, somewhere between Ramey Air Force Base and the City of Arecibo. Las Peliculas would set up headquarters there; then the individual members would infiltrate San Juan and check into different hotels. Each man would try to meet a young lady-preferably an American tourist-and persuade her to accompany him on a cruise. Once they had a boatload, they'd return to Central America for the branding ceremony.

As luck would have it, the six - young debutantes arrived in Arecibo

the same day that Las Peliculas anchored several miles east of the city. The girls made arrangements for lodging, then set out looking for kicks. It wasn't long before they became acquainted with a group of scuba diving enthusiasts. There was a wild beach party, at which marijuana-among other narcotics
-was liberally employed. The party didn't break up until dawn, when everyone passed out on the sand.

It was mid-day when the girls awoke. The scuba divers had long been gone. Now, the girls set out on foot in what they assumed to be the direction of Arecibo. As it was, they went the opposite way—and, by dusk, they were at the campsite of Las Peliculas.

Sandy Pendleton, the young blonde, had more or less assumed command of the group of girls. When they stumbled upon Las Peliculas campsite, she introduced herself to El Diablo and, in halting Spanish, told him who they were and what they were looking for.

"You have strayed far from your quarters," the tattoo terrorists' leader replied amiably. "It would be impossible to find your way back now. I would suggest that you spend the night here with us. Then, tomorrow, we will take you back on our boat."

As far as Sandy was concerned, it sounded like a good-or, in her words, a "kooky"-idea. After all, the girls were looking for kicks, weren't they? And what could be kickier than a band of swarthy Latins, covered with tattoos yet?

El Diablo was delighted with her decision to stay. It was, from his point of view, something like the mountain coming to Mohammed. All along, his group had been planning to infiltrate San Juan with the hope of luring some girls into their lair-and, now, here were six ripe, young American beauties dropping right into their laps.

El Diablo's chief lieutenants, the rotund Pancho and the hawk-nosed Pajaro, cooked an open-fire meal with food from the supply on the boat. Bottles of Puerto Rican rum were broken open and, by the time everyone had finished eating, the entire company was high.

Sandy Pendleton snuggled up next to El Diablo on the cool, sandy beach.

"What do you do for a living?" she asked. "Are you a fisherman?"

"I'm a pirate," he replied, grin
ning.

"Groovy," she said. "I never made it with a pirate before."

El Diablo took her in his arms and covered her mouth with his. "We will remedy that situation at once, senorita," he said.

Meanwhile, back in Florida, the Pendleton family was growing concerned. It had been more than a week since their daughter, Sandra, had left with her girl friends. There had been postcards from Miami, written and addressed in her handwriting. But when they telephoned the hotel at which she was supposed to have been staying (to ask her if she had enough money), they were informed that she had never checked in. Phone calls to the parents of the other girls involved were fruitless. All the parents, it seemed, had been receiving frequent postcards but no one knew where the girls were, or with whom.

Alarmed, the Pendleton family contacted a Miami private detective. Armed with a photograph of the girl and a description of her habits, he began making the rounds. Dade County police had no record of a body being found or an arrest being made involving anyone of the girls' descriptions. But neither was she to be found at any of the hotels or motels, bars or cabana clubs where he checked.

Two days later, he informed the Pendletons that he had been unable to find her. He suggested that they enter a missing persons report with the police. In that manner, he explained, they could be sure that every effort would be made to find her.

The Pendletons decided against a police report on the grounds that it would lead to unfavorable publicity.

"After all," Mr. Pendleton explained to his wife, there's really no reason to believe that something has happened to her. She's disappeared like this before and always turned up no worse for the wear. Who knows? Maybe she and her girl friends took a boat to Jamaica or somewhere. If we send the cops after her and it develops that she's just flitting around, we'll have embarrassed not only ourselves but her and her girl friends also."

Mrs. Pendleton agreed to wait awhile. But, when two days passed and there was no further word from Sandy-except the post cards, which continued to come from Miamishe prevailed upon her husband to employ a different detective agency.

The men he hired this time were the New York private eyes and ex-FBI men, Nat Price and Paul Saunders. The two flew to Palm Beach and obtained from the parents photos of Sandy and the other girls plus a list of all the places in Miami she might visit. They also very fortunately for the girl-obtained her private address book, in which were listed the names, addresses and telephone numbers of a number of her friends.

While Saunders made the customary rounds in Miami, checking with police and retracing the steps of the Miami detective along the Collins

Avenue hotel route, Price telephoned each person listed in the private address book with a Miami address and phone number. On the ninth call, he struck paydirt.

The girl's name was Becky Horne. Like Sandy, she was a young deb from a moneyed family.

It was Becky who had been mailing the post cards for the girls. She had done so, as they had asked her to, ever since they left for Puerto Rico. At the same time, she had been receiving daily letters and postcards from the girls. Then, suddenly, about a week ago, the missives stopped coming. The last one she had received was postmarked Arecibo.

SEXUAL SHENANIGANS "I was getting very worried myself," she told Price. "If you hadn't called, I think I would have contacted Sandy's parents on my own. It isn't like Sandy to stop writing all of a sudden. I think something might have happened to her."

Price rushed to the girl's home. There he took possession of all the letters and postcards. The earliest ones confirmed-in blushing detail-Sandy's sexual shennanigans with a beach boy, a casino croupier and a Puerto Rican entertainer. Subsequent ones went on to say how she was now getting bored with life in San Juan and how she and the girls planned to venture inland in the hope of finding "some way-out adventures with the backwoods natives." The last missive, the card from Arecibo, read:

Becky:

"Have just arrived. Burg looks dead, but it's too early to really say. Have checked into rooming house on outskirts of city. Will write more Tomorrow.

Love, Sandy."

Later the same night, Price and Saunders were on a commercial airliner headed for San Juan. At the airport, they rented a car for the trip inland. On the theory that they wouldn't be able to do much sleuthing until morning, they agreed to spend the night in San Juan-and, to pass the time, they checked all the auto rental agencies. Unless the girls went inland with some newly-made Puerto Rican acquaintances, they probably had rented a car themselves, the detectives reasoned; by this time, the agency from whom they had rented it would have begun to wonder where the vehicle was.

The premise couldn't have been more correct. At the third agency they tried, Price and Saunders found that the girls had indeed rented a car—and that the car was found by police, 'abandoned near Arecibo, more than a week ago.

For the next two days, Price and Saunders went over the small city with a fine tooth comb. The police were cooperative, but unable to shed any light on the situation. The same was true of the operator of the rooming house where the girls had checked in that first night. The girls' luggage was still there, in fact; but the rooming house operator had not seen nor heard from them.

A break in the case came on the second day in the form of a meeting with a young farm boy. He had been fishing off a small pier to the north of the city, he told the detectives. On his way home with his catch, he passed the section of the beach where a wild party was in progress.

The men and women were doing very obscene things with each other," he said. "And the men were very, very funny looking people."

"What was funny about them?"' asked Price.

"They had things all over their bodies," he replied.

"Things? What kind of things?"'

"Peliculas," the boy replied. Pictures!

Much to the pleasant surprise of El Diablo and his cohorts, it was not only possible to lure Sandy Pendleton and her girl friends aboard the cabin cruiser, it was a lead-pipe cinch! After that first night of frantic lovemaking on the beach, the girls seemed only too eager to linger awhile with their tattoo-covered Latin lovers.

SPECIAL PARTY Las Peliculas brought them all aboard and then aimed the vessel toward Guatemala. El Diablo almost turned back when one of the girls let slip the information that their rented car was still parked along the coast. "We will wait while you return it to the rental agency, then we will all leave together," he told Sandy, reasoning that the abandoned vehicle might serve to put police on his tail. "No-it's all right. We made arrangements with a friend of ours," the naive young playgirl lied, "If we are not back tonight, she will return it for us." Believing her, El Diablo told the helmsman to keep on course for Guatemala.

For three days at sea, the girls amused Las Peliculas as royally as any men could hope to be amused. Occasionally, one of them would balk at the suggestion of a voyage into the outri stratospheres of sexual deviation; but, more often than not, they proved only too willing to oblige every taste of their tattooed kidnappers.

"Let things go along as they are going," El Diablo commanded his men, all of whom were sharing the girls. "If they object, do not press the issue. We will wait until we land in Guatemala before we become demanding."

Finally, on the fourth day, the vessel anchored off the Guatemalan coast and Las Peliculas brought their unreluctant captives inland in rowboats.

"And now," El Diablo announced to the girls, "in honor of your having for the first time set foot on Guatemalan soil, we shall have a special party."

A squeal of delight went up from the girls-but it was quickly stifled and replaced by an expression of fear as the girls observed Pancho and Pajaro bringing an array of bizarre apparatus from the boat: Long, metal branding irons, an elaborate brazier and a bagful of coal.

"We are going to have a little barbeque, my dears," grinned El Diablo. "And guess who's on the menu?"

Now that their leader, by his manner, had given the signal that violence was okay, the rank-and-file of Las Peliculas went into action. Pajaro seized one of the girls by the hair and twisted it until she was down on her knees, pleading for mercy.

"Now, rich bitch," he said in English, "kiss my foot."

Her body trembling, she brought her head forward and touched the top of his boot with her lips.

"The other one!" he snapped. She complied. "And now the first one again."

This time, he brought the foot back as she reached for it. Then, with full force, he slammed the toe into her jaw. Blood spurting from her mouth, she fell back onto the ground and spit out her teeth ...

When they heard the young farm boy say the words, "Las Peliculas," Nat Price and Paul Saunders wasted no time. Maybe most American detectives hadn't heard of the Guata mala tattoo terrorists, but Price and Saunders had-and they knew that it could only spell trouble for the girls. A quick telephone call by Price to a private investigator in Guatemala yielded the information that Las Peliculas had vanished after a skirmish with the local police. Conceivably, the informant said, they might have headed for Puerto Rico although the island was usually out of the range of their activities. 'At any rate, he would ask around, if Price wanted him to; he would find out what, if anything, his Guatemalan contacts knew about the group's present whereabouts; and he would phone Price and Saunders as soon as he got any information.

| An hour and a half later, the Guatemala detective had news for them. One of his informers had a pipeline to Las Peliculas' Guatemala headquarters, he said. Earlier in the day, the tattoo terrorists' ship had radioed the headquarters with the message that El Diablo and his boys would be arriving in Guatamala within 24 hours. Moreover, the headquarters had been instructed to gather all land-bound members for a beach ritual.

"Do you know where they conduct - these rituals?" Price asked.

"It could be one of the several beaches near here," the Guatemalan replied. "I can't say which one. But, with a helicopter, I'm sure I could find it—if the money is right."

"The money is right," snapped Price. "Hire a copter and have it waiting. Paul and I will be on the next flight to Guatamala."

Pancho and Pajaro forced the pliant body of Sandy Pendleton into position atop the large, flat stone. Just as her five girl friends had been made to submit to the bizarre branding ritual, it was now her turn. She had pleaded with the fiendish El Diablo, but to no avail; her time had now come, and there was nothing she could do about it.

The two men pried her long, slender legs apart. A third man seized one of the branding irons from the brazier and handed it to El Diablo.

Her body taut with terror, her eyes squeezed shut, Sandy heard the ritual cry of delight from the crowd around the stone. Above it, she heard the strange, mechanical roar-the sound of the approaching helicopter.

"Venga!" she heard Pajaro shout. "Vamonos!" He released his grip on her legs.

"No!" came the harsh reply of El Diablo. "Fuego!".

Sandy Pendleton opened her eyes just in time to see El Diablo, grinning menacingly, brandish the glowing iron into the air and plunge it into the soft, tender flesh inside her thigh. | The searing pain jarring her body, Sandy felt a scream start in her throat and then escape. It was high pitched and agonizing-and, for a moment, she could hardly believe that it was she screaming.

Bullets whined all around her. The screams of the other five girls mingled with the hoarse shouts of the tattoo terrorists. El Diablo whipped a pistol from his belt, dropped behind the stone and began returning the helicopter's fire.

A bullet from the gun of one of Las Peliculas somewhere behind her whizzed by dangerously close to her head. Sandy Pendleton snapped out of her reverie. Sliding off the stone, she lay on her stomach in the sand. Then, burying her face in it, she closed her eyes and tried to blot out what was happening around her.

As the helicopter touched down on the beach, Nat Price and Paul Saunders leaped out, their submachine guns at the ready. Four of the tattoo terrorists had clustered around a slight rise in the sand and were firing at the detectives in concert. Dropping to his knees, Saunders brought the submachine gun to his shoulder and, pulling the trigger, moved it in a slow arc from left to right.

The Latin foursome froze in place, like department store mannequins. Suddenly, little dots of red appeared on their faces-one on a forehead, one on a cheek, one on an eye. They seemed to hang there, suspended like that, for an instant; then their bodies twitched and they fell backward, blood gushing in rivers out of those little red dots on their faces.

Fortunately, four of the girls had the good sense to flee the scene. Now hiding behind a palm tree at the edge of the beach, they were out of the range of fire.

Sandy Pendleton lay motionless alongside the stone. The sixth girl, a tall, bosomy brunette-was the prisoner of Pancho. Using her as a shield, the swarthy Latin advanced, pistol forward, toward Price and Saunders.

The pistol spit out a little flame. Suddenly, Pierce's left arm twitched. The bullet tore into his flesh, and he dropped to one knee.

"Use the damned chopper!" he screamed to Saunders. "It's her or us!"

Saunders pulled his trigger. The burst of shots ripped off the girls wrist-but it also disarmed Pancho behind her. The Latin let go of her and she dropped to the ground, looking disbelievingly at her severed arm. Another burst of bullets from Saunder's gun and Pancho doubled over, his hands around his stomach, a fountain of blood spurting from his back.

There were a few more bursts of submachine gun fire, followed by a pistol shot. Then another burst of submachine gun fire. Then silence.

The silence was almost tangible. Even the ocean seemed to have stopped roaring. Slowly, Sandy Pendleton lifted her head and opened her eyes.

All around her lay the bodies of dead tattoo terrorists. The last group of them had taken to flight down the beach. Price had pursued them and gunned down all eight of them from behind.

Now, there were only the girls and the two detectives. And, rising slowly from behind the stone, his pistol in his hand, El Diablo.

"Give me the gun," Saunders commanded, quietly but firmly.

El Diablo looked into the barrel of the submachine gun pointed at him. Then he looked slowly around the body-littered, blood-spattered beach. His smile seeming to be something he forgot to take off, he glared directly into Saunders' eyes. Then he raised the pistol.

The burst of machine gun fire broke the silence. A triangular pattern of bullets ripped into El Diablo's angular cheek. He stood transfixed for a moment, an expression of incredulity frozen on his face. Then his head snapped back, his body twitched and he fell to the ground. The corpse of the once-smiling El Diablo now had only half a face. The other half was a bloody pulp.

Saunders lowered his submachine gun.

"Live by the sword, die by the sword," he said softly.

Sandy Pendleton lifted herself uncertainly to her feet and stumbled toward him.

They . . . they ... they branded my leg," she said feebly, tears forming in her eyes as she looked at him.

"They should have branded your forehead," said Nat Price, moving in alongside her. Then: "Come on, Paul. Let's get these spoiled brats back home to mom and dad."

Silently, the detectives lead the six girls toward the helicopter ... and home.

THE END

INVEST NOW!
2½ ACRES in TWIN RIVER RANCHOS in NEVADA

$10.00 DOWN
$10.00 MONTHLY
FULL PRICE $495

FAMILY RECREATION
HUNTING: The hunting of your life. Big game species Mule Deer, are abundant. Duck, Quail and Geese are plentiful.

FISHING: A fisherman's paradise. Huge Rainbows, Brook Trout and German Browns abound in Alpine-like lakes and mountain-fed bottom streams.

FOR THE FAMILY: Riding, swimming and all sports. Camping and picnicking sites of unbelievable scenic grandeur.

INSURE YOUR PROFITABLE TOMORROW
Yes, wise investors are buying in TWIN RIVER RANCHOS. America's largest corporations who buy in advance of population explosion are also investing in Nevada. Anaconda Copper has just completed a $32,000,000 plant. North American Aviation, Curtiss-Wright and Kaiser Steel have secured building sites. U.S. Census Bureau Fact: Nevada is the Nation's fastest growing state—8 year population increase, 70%, highest in U.S.A.

TAX RELIEF: No State Income, Gift or Inheritance Tax. The low Real Property Tax is actually limited by the State Constitution.

THE TOTAL COSTS
The full price of the title to your 2½ acre Rancho is only $495.00. Total payment schedule is $10.00 down, and $10.00 per month, including 6% interest. You are not required to do anything to your land. You can live on or vacation on it, or simply watch its value grow, then sell all or part of it for a profit. Your profitable tomorrow is here TODAY in TWIN RIVER RANCHOS.

THE BOOM THAT HAD TO COME IS NOW ON IN NEVADA. Ground floor buyers are reaping fortunes from small initial investments. A factual example of skyrocketing values is Las Vegas, Nevada. Land in Las Vegas that originally sold for $200.00 an acre now sells for $20,000.00 an acre, a profit of 1000%! Buyers who took advantage of low opening prices have become wealthy. The ground floor opportunity of Las Vegas is gone, BUT ANOTHER AREA OF PROPEROUS NEVADA IS NOW BEING RELEASED FOR PUBLIC SALE! This area has such a tremendous growth potential, such a fantastic unlimited future, that wise investors have purchased large acreage. Bing Crosby's ranch was one of the largest ranches in the county. James Stewart is Honorary Sheriff. Yes, the smart experienced investors have sensed the future and are buying TWIN RIVER RANCHOS in Elko County, Nevada.

TWIN RIVER RANCHOS has all of the factors needed to boom...to prosper...to skyrocket its land values. Located on the level, fertile lands of Rich Elko Valley, The Ranchos have the backdrop of the statuesque Ruby Mountains. The sparkling Humboldt River, with its swimming and fishing, actually forms one of the Ranchos' boundaries, and is a valuable asset of the property. Every Rancho fronts on a graded road. The City of Elko, with its long established schools, churches and medical facilities is a friendly neighbor only 12 miles away!

Send $10.00 deposit for each Rancho desired to:
TWIN RIVER RANCHOS Dept. 820
27 Water Street   Henderson, Nevada

NOW! DON'T MISS THIS OUTSTANDING OPPORTUNITY

TWIN RIVER RANCHOS Dept. 820
27 Water Street • Henderson, Nevada

MAIL COUPON TODAY

Yes!—Reserve acreage at TWIN RIVER RANCHOS for me—$495 for each 2½ acre parcel—payable $10 down and $10 a month including 6% interest. No other charges. Send purchase contract and map showing exact location of my holding. You will return my $10 deposit if I request same within 30 days. I enclose $10 deposit for each 2½ acre Rancho desired.

SIZE ACRES	DOWN	PER MO.
2½	$10	$10
5	20	20
7½	30.	30
10	40	40

Name:_____
Address:_____
City:_____ Zone:____ State:_____

Indicate No. of Ranchos ____ Total enclosed $____

LOVE ME TO DEATH
The Incredible Revenge of Colorado Katie

By: Dean W. Ballenger
Art by: Unknown
From: **MAN'S STORY,** August, 1968

Her best weapon was her naked body in a passion plot which marked Gourlay for slaughter.

WHEN KATIE Langford got off the stage in Hay Springs, a hooray cow town on the hoof trail to the Union Pacific's new rail head in Cheyenne, the boys on main street stared like they couldn't believe their eyeballs.

Katie was butt sprung and two quart size in front but she had a face you wouldn't have to put a pillow over and she had a stride that would dingle, a preacher, so everybody naturally watched her sashay over to the marshal's office.

"Shorty," she said to Marshal Matt Dobbs, "where can I find the saloon that Jake Langford, a big red headed cuss from Denver, opened up a couple weeks

ago."

Langford was Katie's husband and she had come to Hay Springs to help him run the boogy part of their saloon business.

Dobbs' eyes avoided Katie's while he said, "Was Mr. Langford something special to you, Miss?"

Katie, suddenly assailed by an intuitive caution against revealing her identity until she found out what was going on, said, The name's Katie Randall, Marshal. What was you gonna say about this big Denver honyocker?"

"Well, Miss Randall, Mr. Langford had a little bad luck. In fact, you could say he ran out of luck. In other words, he ain't with us anymore."

"Who done it?" Katie asked.

"Jeff Gourlay, naturally. That is, one of Gourlay's guns. But I ain't got a shred of hanging proof. The only thing I and everybody else knows is that anybody comes to Hay Springs and tries to start a saloon, he is the same as committing suicide."

Jeff Gourlay, Dobbs explained, owned Hay Springs' three saloons. *Each one of them pays off like a gold mine so he naturally don't want competition."

Dobbs looked into Katie's eyes and seeing their grief, said, "Was Mr. Langford somebody you knowed?"

He sure was," Katie said. "I entertained in his saloon in Denver and when he sold out and come up here I was supposed to come, too." She wiped her tears with a lace handkerchief before she added, "But now that he has went and kicked off it looks like I'm up a tree since I now naturally ain't got the job I was hired for."

"Well, maybe Gourlay will hire you, Miss. That is, if you don't mind working for an 18 karat scudder."

Katie said she couldn't afford to mind. "When a girl is scraping the bottom of her financial barrel she can't afford to be choosy." Then she asked the marshal where she could rent a room. "I gotta pretty up first before I see this Mr. Gourlay."

Ten minutes later, in her room on the second floor of the Hay Springs Hostelry, Katie laid on her bed and wept. She and Langford had operated The Ace of Spades Saloon & Good Time Emporium on Denver's Larimer Street. Competition had been tough. There were four other saloons on the same block so Katie had urged her husband to sell out. "I got my belly full of these butt-pinching city honyockers," she said. "I'll take country boys any day of the week, even if they are a constant boogy worry."

LANGFORD SOLD the saloon to a farmer from Ohio who spent more time trying to peek into Katie's low cut dress than looking at the books.

Katie and Langford decided to launch a saloon and hooray parlor in Hay Springs, a money town on the eastern slope of the Colorado Rockies, northwest of Fort Collins. "With all them herds going through Hay Springs on the way to Cheyenne," Katie said, "we can't help but get well financially."

Three days later Katie and Langford completed purchase of the fixtures and kegs of beer and whiskey they would need for the new enterprise. Then they loaded them into a Conestoga and Langford started driving his mules toward Hay Springs. Meanwhile Katie took the stage to St. Louis, she wanted to visit her ailing mother for a week or two before she joined her husband in Hay Springs. By that time Langford would have rented a building and installed his equipment and got his signs painted. And maybe even opened up for business.

Now, Katie sobbed, her husband was dead and it was her fault. He would have been content to run The Ace of Spades the rest of his life but Katie had wanted money and adventure.

Suddenly the little redhead quit crying. "I'm going to make Gourlay the sorriest honyocker in Colorado," she mumbled, and I'm gonna use my natural good time equipment to do it with!"

The next morning she went to The Square Deal Saloon which was the biggest and most prosperous of Gourlay's three saloons and the one in which he maintained his office.

"I wanta see Mr. Gourlay about an entertainment job," she said with a wink to the bartender, a lard butt whose close-set eyes explored Katie.

Moments later Katie was in Gourlay's office, which was on the second floor above the bar. "I come to Hay Springs to work for Mr. Langford," she said, "I usta work for him in Denver. Howsomever I found out after I got here he ain't in shape to hire nobody. Therefore I would like to work for you, Mister Gourlay."

Gourlay, 52 and wearing prosperous clothes, twisted his graying mustache while his eyes roamed over Katie like a farmer examines an auction heifer. Then, lighting a 50¢ stogie, he said, I got a little rule, Miss Randall: Any lady works for me hasta show me what she has got to work with."

Since you ain't got any other ladies working for you," Katie said, "I know I have just been fed a fable. Howsomever I will be purely glad to give you a sample providing I get this job if it's a pleasin' romp."

Gourlay went to the rail outside his door and yelled down to the bartender that he didn't want to be disturbed. Then he went back into his office and locked the door.

Soon he and Katie were on the horsehair sofa. "'Lord, a'mighty, woman..." Gourlay gasped a little later, "Simmer down. I ain't as young as I used to be."

He was wheezing like a horse with the heaves when Katie finally called it a day. "Woman," he squeaked, "where'd you learn to love like that?"

"It just come naturally," Katie lied. **The only thing I can think of, I betcha the Lord created I and you for each other sexwise and then horsed around all this time before he flang us together so we would appreciate it."

Gourlay hired Katie but he didn't let her work in his saloons. "I ain't going to stand still for every scroungy scudder in Colorado crawling around on you," he said. "You are going to be my personal exclusive bed partner."

He ensconced Katie in his expensive Victorian house on a knoll on the west side of town, a palatial home which he had built for his wife who had died of lung fever six years earlier.

A WEEK AFTER Katie had moved Ainto Gourlay's house Marshal Dobbs, encountering her on Main Street, asked her to come into his office and after she did he said, "Katie, you never did look like no saloon trollop to me so I run a little back track on you. I found out the actual reason you came here."

Katie's face blanched. "Are you gonna tell Gourlay?"

What do you think I am, Katie? Just be careful. He ain't only a mean bugger, he's a tricky son of a bitch."

Katie looked into Dobbs' eyes. They were honest eyes and they didn't waver. "I'll be careful," she said.

"I ain't sure what you got up your sleeve, Katie, but if there is anything I can do to help all you gotta do is ask."

"I am purely obliged, Mr. Dobbs," Katie replied, "but what I've got in mind has to be did by me alone."

In less than a month Katie boogied Gourlay into marrying her. He didn't want to do it, but Katie told him, "I ain't going to be used then flang out when I start getting saggy like I have saw happen a hunnerd times. So either we make it legal or you have had your last romp, Mr. Gourlay."

Since she and Gourlay were in their birthday clothes-Gourlay had thought she was ready for a romp he got as edgy as a stud horse with a spring filly on the other side of the fence. "I could take it from you," he slobbered, staring at Katie's teasers.

"You're talking like a honyocker." Katie said. "A forcible don't hold a candle to a action romp so if you want a decent boogy tonight and in the future, Mr. Gourlay, you know how to get them."

She made Gourlay put on his clothes and go out and get the horseback preacher who had ridden into town the night before, the Rev. Rollie Cooper, who was drinking whiskey in The Square Deal Saloon along with trying to save the souls of the other patrons.

Rev. Cooper was two sheets to the wind when Gourlay brought him to the house along with Moss Steward and Chase Powell, Hay Springs' barber and undertaker, respectively whose function was to serve as witnesses.

Five minutes later Katie was legally Mrs. Jeff Gourlay.

Marshal Dobbs saw Katie on Main Street several days after the wedding. "I'm beginning to get it, Katie," he said, "If Gourlay dies you get it all."

"Not if he dies, Mr. Dobbs. When he dies. I loved my husband. That scudder murdered him."

"Don't do anything I'll have to hang you for," Dobbs said.

"Why? Ain't it your job?"

"I was hoping, Katie, some day maybe I and you..." "I hope so, too," she muttered.

Then she walked away from the little marshal.

"'I set about trying to love Gourlay to death," Katie wrote in her memoirs now in the archives in the Colorado Heritage Society. "I know of no other way to avenge the murder of poor old Jake. I can't do it with a gun. I ain't got the guts to shoot a human being. Besides, I want to do it in a way which wouldn't get me in trouble."

Katie wrote later in her memoirs, "Gourlay liked to done me in again last night. He's a mean man to out romp, but I ain't giving up because I notice he ain't got the durables he used to have and also he has the wheezes when he finally crawls off of me. Therefore I always ask for another romp and if he don't want to do it I physically tease him into it.

"I also am not cooking the kind of meals that builds up a man's heifering ability."

Seven months to the day after Katie euchered Gourlay into marrying her he died suddenly while he was loving. "I crawled out from under the big lout," she wrote in her memoirs,

and went and got Doctor Ira Campbell. I wanted Doc to noise it around that Gourlay had kicked off of a heart attack so the local honyockers wouldn't think I had put the Indian sign on him."

The day of the funeral, after Gourlay was buried in Hay Springs' cemetery, Katie went to Marshal Dobbs' office. "I'm going to need a gent I can trust," she said, "to help me run them 3 saloons my late husband left

me."

"Is that all you're going to need, Katie," Dobbs said with a wink.

"Nope, it sure ain't," she replied.

She locked the door and pulled down the shades and showed him what else she needed on the buffalo-hide settee back of his desk.

THE END

A "BEATING-UP" TURNED THIS WEAKLING INTO A CHAMP!

Charles Atlas — "World's Most Perfectly Developed Man"

One night a frail 97-lb., 15-year-old youth was making his way home through the tough waterfront section of New York City. Suddenly, without warning, a brutal hoodlum loomed up out of the dark, and beat him senseless. That night the young man made a solemn vow: "Never will I let any man hurt me again."

The years ahead were to prove how well he kept that vow! For the name of that skinny youth was Charles Atlas — and he lived to become internationally famous as "The World's Most Perfectly Developed Man," performing feats of strength that amazed the whole world!

The day after that beating, Charles Atlas began trying every exercise he had ever heard of. Then one day, visiting New York's famed Bronx Zoo, he asked himself: "How does the *tiger* keep in physical condition? You never see *him* with a barbell!"

Atlas Discovers the Secret!

He saw how the tiger exercised by stretching its muscles, one against the other. From this, he worked out the amazing "Dynamic-Tension" system of muscle-building that was to make him famous.

Within 12 months, Atlas had doubled his weight. He decided to help all weak, underdeveloped men who suffered as he had. So he made his amazing secret of "Dynamic-Tension" — the system that uses no weights or apparatus — available to men all over the world. Thousands have benefited from his remarkably effective system.

And, as the fame of Charles Atlas spread, he was challenged to perform many thrilling feats of strength. Once he pulled six automobiles, chained together, for a mile. Another time he towed a 72½-ton railroad car 112 feet along the tracks with a rope!

A far cry from the days of that 97-pound weakling who sobbed his way home after a beating, made a vow that changed his whole life — and since has changed the lives of so many others!

Charles Atlas Towing Broadway Limited Observation Car 112 ft!

I Take OLD Bodies and Turn Out NEW Ones!

Check the Kind of NEW BODY You Want RIGHT IN THE COUPON BELOW . . . and I'll Show You How EASILY You Can Have It!

I'M NO MAGICIAN. Making healthy and handsome HE-MEN out of weaklings — turning "skin and bones" or flabby fat into SOLID MUSCLE — is simply my job. But my secret *does* work like "magic."

Do you want broader shoulders — a magnificent "barrel" chest — more powerful arms and legs — a mid-

section lined with solid-as-steel muscle? It's all waiting for you. Just check what you want — RIGHT IN THE COUPON BELOW. I'll show you how I can give it to you!

From "Mouse" to MAN!

You wouldn't believe it but I myself used to be a 97-lb. weakling. Fellows called me "SKINNY." Girls made fun of me behind my back. Then I discovered my remarkable muscle-building secret — "Dynamic-Tension." It turned me from a "bag of bones" into a barrel of muscle! And I felt so much better, so much *on top of the world* in my big, new, husky body, that I decided to devote my whole life to helping *other* fellows change themselves into "*perfectly developed men.*"

"Dynamic-Tension" Works Fast!

My secret — *Dynamic-Tension* — is the NATURAL, easy method you can practice right in the privacy of your own room — JUST 15 MINUTES EACH DAY — while you build up SOLID MUSCLE in all of the RIGHT PLACES — gain the kind of handsome and healthy build that women admire and men respect.

I give you no gadgets or contraptions. You simply use the SLEEPING muscle-power in your own body almost unconsciously every minute of the day — walking, bending over, even sitting at your table or desk!

ARE YOU Skinny, Weak and run down? Always tired? Nervous? Fat and flabby? Want to lose or gain weight? WHAT TO DO ABOUT IT is told in my FREE BOOK

Charles Atlas Holder of title "The World's Most Perfectly Developed Man"

Prize Trophy Given Away Be the envy of friends! Win handsome trophy, over 1½ feet high!

FREE My 32-Page Book is Yours Not $1.00 or 10¢ — But FREE

SEND NOW for my book describing my famous method. 32 Pages, packed with actual photographs and valuable advice. Shows what "Dynamic-Tension" has done for others. Page by page it shows what I can do for YOU. Just glancing through it may mean the turning point in your life — and its yours absolutely FREE! Check the kind of body you want below.

CHARLES ATLAS, Dept. 933, 115 East 23rd St., New York, N. Y. 10010.

CHARLES ATLAS, DEPT. 933, 115 East 23rd Street, New York, N. Y. 10010

Dear Charles Atlas: Here's the kind of Body I Want:

(Check as many as you like)
- [ ] Broader Chest and Shoulders
- [ ] More Powerful Arms and Grip
- [ ] Slimmer Waist and Hips
- [ ] More Powerful Leg Muscles
- [ ] More Weight — Solid — in the Right Places
- [ ] Better Sleep, More Energy

Send me absolutely FREE a copy of your famous book showing how "Dynamic-Tension" can make me a new man. 32 Pages crammed with photographs, answers to vital health questions, and valuable advice. I understand this book is mine to keep and sending for it does not obligate me in any way.

Print
Name...Age......
Address...
City.......................State.......Zip Code........

In England: Charles Atlas, Chitty St., London, W.1

MY WILD ESCAPE FROM THE
MAFIA'S ORGY ISLAND PARADISE

By: Bart Handley as told to Mark Brand
Art by: Norman Saunders
From: **MAN'S STORY,** December, 1973

They stocked their playground with a lush collection of nakjed playmates who'd do anything for laughs — even love a guy to death. It could have been fun except —

MARIA CICCIO took off her blouse, stepped out of her skirt, removed her bra and worked her panties down over sun-bronzed legs. She was ready. She came across the room toward me, her firm breasts dancing, hips swaying, her face bright with a big professional smile. Her body was soft and warm.

I'd paid her 1,000 lire to use it, but I had other things on my mind. My hands settled on the small of her back. "You saw a girl here yesterday?"

Maria's lips pecked at my face and neck. "What girl?" Her thighs dug in hard.

"Blonde. American. I have to know." "Forget her, signor. She is beyond reach." Maria urged me to her bed. She fell back on it smiling. "On Lipari you don't ask questions.

I sat beside her. I rubbed her belly gently. "Will you tell me where she is for twenty thousand lire?"

She sat up quickly. "For that much I will show you." She pulled me to her window, pointed to a tower that was barely visible in the darkness. "That is Via Calogera. Meet me there in an hour."

"Why not now?"

Her hand shot to her throat. "No, signor, if they knew they would send their boia to give me the lupara sickness." She pressed close. "You will not greet me when I pass you. Just follow me." She snapped her fingers. "The money."

I counted out the bills and then left.

A few minutes later I stood under the tower and waited. The island was Lipari, north of Sicily, and known as the capi mafiosi's playground. Lipari wasn't a resort area like Taormina, but chieftains came here for sun, fun and privacy, the kind of privacy you needed when the program called for a sexual binge.

Against sound advice, a thoughtless girl named Cindy Graham had rented a launch on Stromboli, where she'd been staying with her uncle, and had come to Lipari alone. And now I was searching for her.

I saw a figure dressed in black coming into the square. It was Maria. She kept to the shadows of the buildings. Then she was beside me, a black veil over her face. I said, "Okay, show me."

The veil came up. The face wasn't Maria's. It was a man's. *Signor, there is a gun pointed at you. Stand perfectly still."

Another figure emerged from the shadows. A pair of hands went over me. I was told to walk north at a normal pace.

My fists had knotted with rage. The black-haired bitch Maria had conned me. I'd been a fool to trust her.

I was taken to a bleached villa on a hill outside of town. Secluded. Guards met us at the door. I was frisked again. Inside, I was met by a fat man. His sneer displayed a row of stubby teeth. "You gave Maria twenty thousand lire just for information about this American girl. Why?"

**She's important." "To whom?" "Me." "You her lover?" I nodded. The fact was I'd never met Cindy Graham, but I'd had orders not to divulge my client's name if I were caught. His brother-in-law was too well-known-a mogul in the Hunt-HughesGetty class.

The bait dangled in front of me had been a fee of $50,000. One of the guards handed the fat man my ID. The card had my name on it and a New York address. Nothing else. He turned it over in his hands and grunted, "Follow me."

WE ENTERED the patio. Five hard-eyed men stared at me.

Sicilian brotherhood. Capi mafiosi. Young, unsmiling women circulated among them, serving drinks, making them comfortable.

At one corner of the patio there was a blonde girl leaning heavily against the potted palm. Most of her clothes had been torn off and her flesh was bruised. Her hair hung in front of her face.

"Cindy!" I started towards her. I knew what the fat man had in mind and I wanted to reach her fast. But two guards jumped in front of me.

Cindy was dragged away from the plant and made to face me. The Mafia chief stood between us. He glanced at my ID again. "Tell me your lover's name."

The girl was puzzled. She stared at me, then lowered her eyes.

There was a sudden explosion of pain at my mouth. I reeled under the fat man's quick punch. I heard him growl, "Liar!" But that was all. Fists came at me from every direction. I heard Cindy scream. A knee came up into my face. I was lifted to my feet and slammed against the wall. My guts were pounded by a vicious flurry of blows that doubled me. The knee came up again, harder this time, snapping my head back. Vaguely, I heard somebody say, "Don't kill him. I have to know who sent him." Then I went down on the hard tile floor and passed out.

A scream brought me around. I had the taste of blood in my mouth. My guts ached. I raised my head for a better look at what was going on.

I didn't like what I saw.

Two of the fat chief's assistants held Cindy's arm. The big man stood in front of her. She must have been slapped hard because her cheeks were scarlet. His big hands were on her shoulders now. They moved up to her neck. He worked her head from side to side, his hands rubbing her face and throat and slipping into her hair. "Tell us about yourself, Cindy. What've you got to lose? You rich, maybe? How come that creer lied? Your old man a big politician, or something?"

The girl sobbed. She was so scared she couldn't have talked if she'd wanted to. But that didn't cut any ice with her tormentor. He smashed her across the face. Her knees buckled. She was held up. Tears rolled down her cheeks. Thick fingers dug into her cleavage and curled around her bra. Cindy struggled. One quick snap of the wrist left her naked to her navel. The Mafia chief stared at her nudity for a moment, then brought his hands up to touch her. She recoiled, gasping at the man's brazen handling of her.

I put my hands under my body to lift myself up, but couldn't. I'd taken more of a beating than I'd thought. I sagged down on the tile and that was when I saw what was happening.

It was something never seen by anyone except those of high rank in the so-called Honored Society.

The capi mafiosi were taking part in a drunken, Roman-type sex orgy which can only be hinted at. Even through my dimmed vision I could tell that some of the loveliest women in the Mediterranean were here. All were naked. Each chieftain had one or two fawning over him. They were on chairs and on the floor. The women threw themselves at the men, agreeing to any depravity. I could guess that many of the beauties needed favors. Maybe a life spared, or a job for a destitute relative. A sudden scream brought my attention back to Cindy.

SHE HAD been thrown to the floor. The two men held her

shoulders down. The fat man stood over her. Cindy saw what he was doing now and her face paled. She screamed again. The men leaned heavily on her to keep her from moving. They looked up at their boss to see what was delaying him. He made flicking motions with his fingers. "Get off her." The men faded. He sneered down at her. "Relax." He spread his hands out in front of him, glaring. "Why did you have to come poking around?"

The remark shook me. I'd figured she had been snatched. So had my client. We both should have known better. The Mafia frowns on kidnaping. Too risky. Besides, the men here were too big to bother with grabbing a girl off the street. The truth was that Cindy Graham had poked her nose into a place where it didn't belong, and now she'd got more kicks than she'd bargained for.

The chief waddled across the patio and sank heavily into a chair. He downed a whiskey, frowning, then stuffed a black cigar into his mouth. He waved his arm toward Cindy. "What the hell am I gonna do with her?"

One of his cronies sat up. "Send her back, Lou. She's too hot."

"I can't. She'll talk her head off. She saw too much." Lou turned in his chair. "Hey, all of you-out!" The naked women didn't question the order. They filed into the house and shut the glass door. The men got up and moved over to where Lou sat. There was no talk for awhile. The men paced slowly, puffing on cigars.

Lou broke the silence. "She's got us all fixed. So's he." "Main thing is, Lou, we got to keep our hands clean."

Another one said, "They came in separate launches. We'll have to get rid of them, too."

Lou said, "Tomorrow I'll round up some boys." He screwed his face up tight.

"After dark, Lou. And make sure the boys take 'em way out. I don't want no bodies floating back."

The fat man nodded. He snapped his fingers and his two assistants hustled over to him. "Tie that creep up and get him out of my sight."

Fortunately, Cindy was too far away from the men to hear their decision to kill us. She was still on the floor. She sobbed quietly into her hands. The capi mafiosi wandered back to their chairs. My wrists and ankles were bound so that I was bent backwards like a bow. I was dragged through the glass door. The naked women were in the room waiting for permission to return to the patio.

Suddenly, the front door burst open and a woman came through it screaming, "You killed him! Why? Why?"

Lou pushed through the glass door to see what the commotion was all about. The woman fought off the guards and rushed up to the chieftain.

I could see her now. It was Maria Ciccio.

She pounded the big man's chest, sobbing hysterically, "My father was only an old man... why did you have to kill him?"

Lou shoved her away from him. She toppled to the floor. He brushed himself off, sneering: "Get her the hell out of here." Then he ordered the other women to get back to the patio.

I didn't see anymore. I was dragged into an anteroom and the door was closed. I started to work on the knots right away. but the position of my body made it almost impossible for me to make any headway. After twenty minutes of struggling I gave up.

The door opened noiselessly. A pair of sun-tanned legs stepped across the threshold and the door was closed.

My visitor was Maria.

SHE KNELT beside me in the dark. She was close enough

for me to smell the aroma of her perfume. Quiet sobs issued from her throat. "My father ... he was a big man in the Mafia... but in his old age he talked too much, perhaps ... but they did not have to shoot him down like a dog ..." She worked on the knots. "It pains me that I betrayed you for them. Take my advice, signor. Get away. They will kill you, too... and also for letting you escape."

She stood up when the rope was off. She opened the door a crack and peeked out. Then she left.

The room outside was empty. I could see the patio. The orgy was still in progress. My only chance of reaching Cindy would be from the far side. I slipped back into the anteroom and went to the window. I opened it and climbed out. Crouched low, I ducked into the wooded area beside the villa and headed for the rear section of the patio.

Cindy hadn't moved much. She sat leaning against a potted plant, her eyes turned away from the sordidness. I went down on my belly and crawled to the balustrade. I slid over it and crouched behind one of the plants.

I'd been lucky, so far. Lou and the others were too busy with their women to notice my presence. I crept up behind Cindy. I put one arm around her middle and the other across her mouth to keep her from crying out. She went rigid with fear. I dragged her behind a large plant. She relaxed when she saw me. I took my hand away. She started to say something. I covered her mouth again.

I went to the balustrade and scaled it. Cindy followed my example, hugging the marble as she threw one leg over. I raised my hands and eased her down to the ground. Now it was just a matter of getting to the launch, about a mile away.

The woods gave us good cover. We skirted the town and headed for the waterfront, dark and empty at this hour. I spotted my launch at the dock. We ran to it at top speed. I helped Cindy on board and went to the helm."Hold it!"

I SPUN TO the sound of the voice. Two men came up from the cabin. They held black automatics. They were Lou's assistants, the same two who'd tied me up.

I sank down heavily on the helmsman's chair.

The men were puzzled. They wanted to know how I'd gotten loose. I didn't tell them. They thought Cindy had helped me, but they nixed that idea. Then one of them growled, "Maria. She was there tonight."

"Yeah, for the pay-off. She's always had it in for Lou since her old man got the lupara sickness. That bitch did it,

I didn't answer. The question that bothered me was what these characters were doing on my boat. I found out on the way back to the villa. They'd been planting dynamite charges in the holds of both launches. The blasts would sink the boats and Cindy and me with them.

The fat chief was at the front door when we were dragged back to the villa. His face was red with rage. "How'd it happen?" he asked between clenched teeth.

"Maria," one of the guards grunted.

Lou grunted, "Get her. Right now," he sneered. "Same way her old man got it."

The car trunk was opened and a shotgun taken from it. Lou nodded his approval. Murder by shotgun was the traditional method in Sicily. The mafiosi loaded their own shells with pellets about the size of buckshot-filled into a pyramid-shape known as Lupara. The victim of lupara sickness was literally cut to pieces.

Lou's assistants drove off. The guards on the door trailed behind us as we followed the fat man into the villa. We climbed three flights of stairs. Lou pushed into an empty room. The guards were ordered to tie me up.

After they were finished with me, they went to Cindy. Lou snapped, "No. Get Out! Leave the rope here.

The men left. Lou rubbed his fat hands together. His eyes narrowed to slits. Cindy backed up to a wall. The Mafia chief started towards her, slowly, his fingers spreading. "I'm gonna finish what I started downstairs."

Cindy shook her head. "No... please ..."

Lou spread his heavy arms wide. "You should've thought of that before you got nosey, kid. You play with fire, you're gonna get burned." He pointed to the floor. "I got five brothers downstairs all want a crack at you before tomorrow night." He grabbed her wrists. "Fight me, kid... make me work for it."

Cindy wrenched free and ran to the door. It had been locked from the outside. She turned to the fat man, and through her sobs and sniffles she screamed, "You're a filthy, disgusting pig!"

Lou roared with harsh laughter. "Keep it up, blondie. Let's see what kind of spunk you got." He closed in on her again. She beat him on the face with her fists, but it didn't stop him. He crushed her against the wall. His forearm went to her throat and he used his free hand to rip off the remnants of material that covered her.

As soon as he pulled his arm away from her throat, Cindy darted away. She ran to the window and flung it open. She put one leg on the sill. I yelled at her to get back. Then Lou grabbed her and pulled her away. He held her against his body. Both of his hands moved over her sensitive areas freely. She struggled. Her legs flailed wildly. She screamed at him to leave her alone. He lowered her until her feet touched the floor, then he wrapped her hair around his hand and snapped her head back. "Don't move, kid. You could break your neck."

Cindy was helpless now. She knew that just a little more pressure on Lou's part could crack her spine or neck. The fat man stared down at her body. He touched her breast, then slid his hand down to her belly. Cindy didn't fight him. She was afraid to move.

I WATCHED THE sneer on the fat man's lips fade. He dropped the girl to the floor. He stared down at her, his loose mouth drooling. Cindy made an effort to squirm away, but he dropped fast, locking her to the floor. She screamed again. Her fists beat the floor and her head rolled from side to side. Lou forced himself between her thighs. She pounded his head with her fists. Then suddenly her body jerked and her mouth opened in a long, car-piercing scream. Her arms went limp and she passed out.

When he was done, Lou tied her up, checked the knots that held me, then growled to the guards to open the door. He was gone. I heard a key turn in the lock.

Cindy came to and shuddered. I rolled over to her, shifting my body until I could reach the knots on her wrists. After she was freed I told her to do the same for me.

"What good will it do?" she moaned, hopelessly. "We can't escape."

"I have an idea. Just get these ropes off."

She struggled with the knots. "It's stupid to even try."

I urged her to hurry.

Minutes later I had the ropes tied together. I dropped one end out the window and lowered it. No good. The rope was a good thirty feet too short. I yanked it up and went to the door. A look through the keyhole told me we had an armed guard outside. Lou wasn't taking any chances.

Cindy slumped to the floor, whining: "I told you it was hopeless."

"Shut up."

"What were they saying about dynamite on our boats? They're going to kill us, aren't they?"

"What the hell do you think?"

I'd blurted it out. I glanced quickly at her to see how she'd taken it. She leaned against the wall and sighed, "I suppose I knew it. When?"

**Tomorrow night." "I was a fool." "What made you do it?" I asked.

She shrugged. "Curiosity. I'd heard a lot about Lipari. I wanted to see it for myself."

"What exactly did you see?"

"I was at the car-ferry. Big black sedans had arrived from Messina. I followed them here on foot." She lowered her eyes. "I spied on their meeting. It was easy. There were no guards outside."

I grunted. "You could've been shot on sight."

She dropped her head on her arms. "I thought the whole thing was terribly overrated."

"If you mean the Mafia, that was mistake number one."

Cindy went to the window. "I know that now. Did my uncle send you?"

"Yeah."

The sky had brightened. I saw four men coming up the road from town.

Cindy said, "Are you a detective?"

"Not quite." The men hurried into the house. They were probably our boia (executioners). The two who were assigned to kill Maria hadn't returned yet. I remembered Lou's remark about his brothers coming up here for a crack at Cindy. I grabbed her. "Get down on the floor!"

"What for?" "'Shut up and do as I say!"

She jerked away from me. Her lips trembled. "I'm sick of being man-handled."

I pulled her close. "Get this. I'm going to save my skin and I don't give a damn who I hurt to do it." I kicked her feet out from under her and she went down. I wrapped the rope around her body.

"I don't understand."

"You don't have to," I growled at her. "Just stay put."

I sat on the far side of the door and waited. The sun was high when a key turned in the lock. I got up and flattened myself against the wall. A Mafia chieftain entered. He was alone. The guard closed the door and locked it.

The man stood over Cindy. He said. "Lou tells me he had fun with you. Now it's my turn."

He had his coat half off when the side of my palm came down hard on his neck. He slumped. I caught him, put him on the floor and went through his pockets. He was clean. No weapon of any kind. Lousy luck.

I took the rope off Cindy. I heard a car pulling up outside. I went to the window. The men with the shotgun had returned. They got out, shaking their heads at Lou. "Couldn't find her, one said. I went to the door, braced myself and knocked twice.

It opened. I lunged at the guard. He didn't have time to bring his rifle up. My first blow caught him on the chin. The second went to his gut. He doubled over. I brought my knee up. He sagged. I grabbed his rifle and motioned to Cindy to follow me.

WE HURRIED down the stairs. I kept my fingers on the trigger, ready to blast anybody who got in our way. The only escape route open to us was through the cellar. There had to be an underground passageway leading away from the house. Most villas had them.

The cellar was dark and damp. I moved cautiously. Excited talk coming from the upper rooms indicated the mafioso had found out what had happened. There'd be men all over the house and grounds now. I'd hoped for a little more time. My luck had run from bad to worse.

Then the cellar door opened and a beam of light played over us. Somebody yelled, "They're down here!"

I snapped off two rounds. The first killed the light, the second must have hit flesh because there was a scream of pain. Cindy and I crouched low and followed the stone wall. Another light came on and fixed us. A shot chipped stone above my head. I answered it with two bullets but both were wild. Heavy footsteps sounded on the stairs. I fired at them and heard a thud. The light had gone out.

Then another beam exposed us. I squeezed the trigger and nothing happened. The rifle was empty. Cindy grabbed my arm. "Look!" I followed her pointing finger to a hole in the wall. We ran to it and plunged in.

It was a water duct. The other end probably opened near the shore. If we could make it to the sea we could swim to the launch. I felt that we had a chance now, that we'd done the impossible. I dropped the rifle and held Cindy's hand. I started off at a fast run, tugging her when she attempted to slow down. It was totally black in the tunnel and we had to run in a crouched position, but after a minute or two a speck of light was visible at the other end. The girl broke my grip on her hand. grabbed her. "We've got to keep going!"

I can't..."

My fingers circled her wrist. I forced her to run. The tunnel opening grew bigger. I could hear the breakers crashing on the rocks. Cindy balked again. I jerked her arm. "Come on! We're almost there." She nodded, unable to speak. We were both exhausted. But we had no choice. We had to make it.

Now the opening was only a few yards ahead of us. We got our second wind and made a last desperate spurt. We hit the burning sunlight and stopped dead. All our hopes of escape came crashing down on us as we faced the four boia who'd been commissioned to execute us.

The sudden turn of events was too much for Cindy. She collapsed on the ground, sobbing uncontrollably.

I stood still, breathed deeply to get some strength back. The men weren't armed, but they had that look in their eyes that said they were going to give me a good working over before they brought us back to the villa a second time.

They spread out, then moved in slowly. I tried to keep all of them within my range of vision. Beyond them, I could see the soapy breakers, less than 100 yards away. We'd almost made it. It was a lousy, rotten feeling. Rage rumbled within me. I swung at them, stiff-legging one in the groin, karate chopping another. I took a vicious blow to the face that snapped my head, but only served to increase my savage urge to wax as many of these characters as I could before I went down.

Two of them pounded me to my knees. I picked up a rock and smashed it into a sneering face. Blood spurted...a jawbone cracked. I jumped up and slammed the rock against one guy's mouth and heard his teeth break. The one I'd kicked in the groin was back for more. I hit him in the eye with the rock, shattering his orb. The last one charged me with a switchblade. I brought my foot up between his legs. There was an ugly squishing sound. His eyes rolled back in their sockets. I slammed the rock against his head. He hit the ground and didn't move.

IT WAS ALL over. I staggered over to Cindy and urged her to stand up. "Come on. kid... There's still a chance for us ..."

She fell into my arms. I held her close to me and tried to stop her trembling. She sobbed, "It's a nightmare... A horrible nightmare...

"It'll be over soon." I led her to the beach. We walked into the water. I turned to look at the villa. It was peaceful. Lou was probably inside waiting for his boia to bring us back. He had a surprise coming to him.

We swam a few yards out, then headed for the town's waterfront section. I didn't press Cindy to hurry because we had a good mile of swimming to do. Still, she had trouble staying afloat. I held her up most of the way.

At the launch's stern I let go of her and boosted myself to the deck. I leaned over the gunwhale, grabbed Cindy's hands and hauled her aboard. She was draped across my lap and smiling for the first time. Her arms were around my neck. She pulled herself up and kissed me.

"A real touching scene."

The sound of the voice startled us. Cindy screamed. I could feel blood draining out of my head.

It was the fat man. He held a blue steel automatic on us and his guttural laugh grated my ears. He waved the gun toward the villa. "They said I was crazy to come down here and sit in the boat." The laugh died. He tapped his chest. "Know why I'm on top in this racket?" He came closer, his eyes snapping from Cindy to me, his lower lip hanging loose. "Because I don't underestimate my enemies, that's why!"

There was a shot. I couldn't see where it had come from. Lou's pig eyes widened. His body stiffened. Blood bubbled up in his mouth and spilled over. He dropped to his knees.

Behind him, Maria stood in the hatchway. Her face was a mask of hate. She raised her gun and fired again. She walked up to Lou, stood over him and emptied the gun into his body.

Her cheeks were wet with tears. She knelt beside the dead man and touched one of the wounds. Cindy started to go to her, but I held her back. Maria had begun the ritual of the vendetta. We had no right to interfere.

The girl put her red-stained fingers to her lips and looked up at the sky. "In this way may I drink the blood of the man who killed you, my father."

She stood up and tossed her gun overboard. I hauled in our lines, started the engine and told Cindy to go below. I eased the launch into open water. Maria stood beside me. She cried, "Go down there with her. I'll take the wheel, signor." "You'll be alright?" She smiled. "I'll never be all right now. They'll find me no matter where I go.

I went down to Cindy. She was naked behind a bath towel. I stripped off my wet clothes and yanked the towel out of her hands. "Hey, that's not nice," she laughed, trying to grab it from me. I held it high. She came close. Her breasts rubbed against me. I dropped the towel and put my arms around her. Her warmth flooded me with desire. Her smile faded and our lips smashed together. She broke away from my lips, threw her head back. I kissed her throat and maneuvered her to a bunk.

She looked up at me. "How long does it take to get to Stromboli?" "Who gives a damn?"

END

"NEW!" PORTABLE MACHINE! STAMPS BIG PROFITS!

WE Supply Everything... You just make money!

This remarkable new machine "engraves" lifetime Social Security metal plates, Door/Name plates, Identification Tags and Plates, Medicare plates, and over 100 different Social Security, Identification, Fraternal and Religious Perma-Cards, Pet Tags, Key Protector Tags, Medical Tags . . . and you can operate it easily anywhere you happen to be!

NO EXPERIENCE NEEDED! AGE NO BARRIER!

We supply all you need . . . it's up to you how much money you can make. You can work through agents and we'll provide the ads and materials for you. If you like Mail Order, we'll provide circulars already proven successful. Or we can supply you with a special Fund-Raising Plan. Or, tell you how to place order-getting counter display boards in local stores for high volume, fast profit! Since the machine is portable, you can "set up shop" out of your car, or use your kitchen table as your "factory." Any method you choose is a proven one, and should make you BIG MONEY as a spare-time or full-time business. All methods of operation are thoroughly covered in our Free "Big Money" book.

FREE SOCIAL SECURITY PLATE!

Send the coupon for Free lifetime-metal Social Security Perma-Card and Carrying Case, with complete details of this unusual home business opportunity today!

FREE PICTURE CATALOG
(ALL ITEMS, SUPPLIES & EQUIPMENT)

MAIL NOW FOR FREE BOOK

AN "ARSENAL" OF SALES AIDS TO HELP YOU MAKE MORE MONEY! WITH YOUR STAMPING KIT . . .

Besides Mail Order Circulars, Counter Display Boards, Fundraising Forms and mats for ads, agent supplies, Social Security Earnings Post Cards, Stationery, etc., you will receive a beautiful Attache Case and Deluxe Kit for the professional appearance, a Display Book with actual samples of every plate, tag, etc., . . . everything you need to set up a moneymaking business of your own.

PERMA PRODUCTS, Inc.
Dept. X-11
275 N.E. 166th Street
North Miami Beach, Fla. 33162

Types of Plates
Social Security . Medical
Identification . Auto
Pet . Key . Door

FREE SUPPLY CATALOG!

PERMA PRODUCTS, Inc. Dept. X-11
275 N.E. 166th Street
North Miami Beach, Fla. 33162
Please rush a FREE Sample metal Social Security Perma-Card, Carrying Case, FREE 24-page "Big Money" book, and postcard to get record of my Social Security earnings, plus complete details on how I can make big money in my Perma home business. FREE Supply Catalog! No salesman will call.
(Please Print)
Name _____
Address _____
City _____
State _____ Zip _____

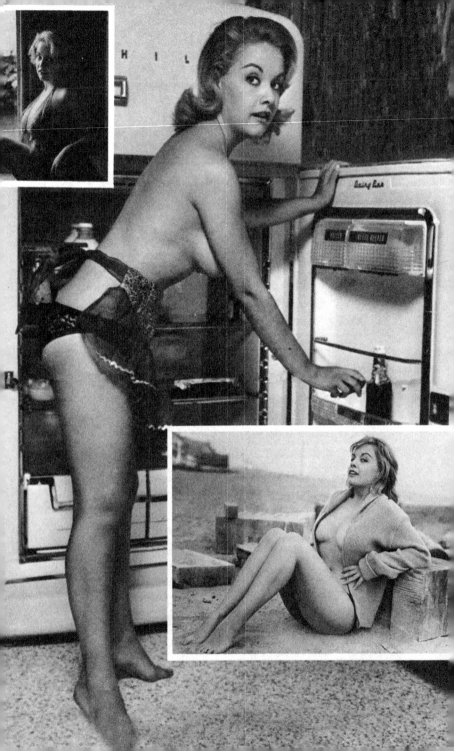

Blonde of the Month

JUDY CROWDER

Next time you see our blonde charmer Judy Crowder, you may be watching your TV set. She's auditioning for spot commercials. Judy has acted in summer stock and is taking singing, dancing and drama lessons. She's determined to make it in show biz...

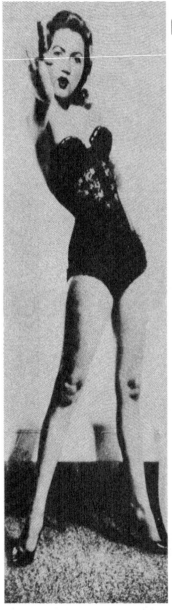

Betsy Compton says:

'I Like Being With A Guy Who Knows What He Is Doing'

I consider myself a normal young woman, I like movies, TV, good shows, and I'm not ashamed to say, I *love* sex. I'm not like a lot of girls you know who consider natural relationships with the opposite sex taboo. There's no sense kidding around, sex is great and I'm out to get the most out of it.

A book publisher that I know quite well gave me a book that he recently published just a few months ago. It is called The American Handbook of Sex and Marriage. After reading it from cover to cover (I couldn't put it down!), I came to the conclusion that this is the greatest book of its type that I had ever read, and believe me, I studied up on my sex pretty thoroughly. After hearing my enthusiastic approval of his book, the publisher asked me if I would do a written "commercial" about it.

I won't bore you with a lot of statements that doctors make about sex, except to say that it is pretty well known that most people aren't getting as much out of their sex life as they could. To me, this fact is really a shame! Personally I found that even with my experience, and I've had quite a bit, I learned quite a few interesting things from the AHSM. As a matter of fact, I kept referring to it as often as I feel is necessary. Before I go out on a date, or to a party, you can be sure that I go over the book, because then I know that I'm ready for *anything*.

For a man or woman, this book really has the answers. Frankly, all I'd have to know is that a fellow has read the American Handbook and I'll go out with him in a minute. This may sound exaggerated, but I like the feeling of being with a guy who *knows what he's doing*. And this is the book to teach you. And I don't want to forget about the married couples. If you think that things are becoming a little dull in respect to sex, get ahold of this book and see what the difference is after you've read it.

This book isn't for deadheads... it's for people that want to learn, and want to know that sex is something that can always be exciting and fulfilling. If you want The American Handbook on Sex and Marriage, all it costs you is $3.00. That's a small price for what this book can mean to you. Besides, if you aren't satisfied (and I can't believe that *anyone* wouldn't be with this book) your full $3.00 will be quickly and cheerfully refunded. You can get the book by sending your $3.00 to Betsy Compton, care of Jalart House, Inc., Post Office Box 175, Port Chester, New York. (Sent in plain wrapper and you must be over 21).

Hurry and get the book today and I know that you'll be as enthusiastic about it and about your new sex life as I am.

DEATH WATCH OF THE 2ND PLATOON

By: Sgt. Wayne Stevens
Photos by: Unknown
From: **KEN FOR MEN,** May, 1957

We were 27 men, on foot, cut off from our lines, with a whole Red division on our tails.

You just needed two words to describe the basic combat tactic in the
In the early days of the Korean War—"bug out." I don't know what
GI dreamed them up to describe what the textbooks call a "strategic
withdrawal" or "tactical retreat," but they fitted, believe me. And I
didn't need any diagrams to know that's what we'd better do that steaming hot day late in July, 1950.

The North Koreans had slammed over the 38th Parallel less than four weeks before. They rolled back everything that stood in their way; in the beginning there wasn't much to stand up to 'em.

By the time my outfit, the 5th Regt. of the 1st Cavalry Division, was jerked off Occupation duty in Japan and landed at Pohang-dong, American forces were hanging on by their teeth down around Taegu.

At first, that July morning wasn't much different than the others. We were getting shot at and men were dying. The enemy had infiltrated our positions on the high ground alongside a small river. Now they were pouring fire down on the whole damn battalion.

But it wasn't just the enemy right there on our necks that we had to worry about. About four miles away were the lead elements of a full armored division.

You don't need a West Point education to know what comes next in that situation. The company commander put the idea into action. "Stevens," he yelled over the crack of small arms fire.

I peered out from behind my private rock and saw him back aways in what could laughingly be called the company CP. It was just another couple big rocks and a tree. I ducked across an open space and skidded up to him.

There was no need for any fancy briefings. I knew the situation as well as he did, it was miserable. "You set up a 'bug out' line down here," he said. "Cover while we pull out Dog and Baker companies. We won't take long moving out. Hang on and then grab the last vehicle out. I'll line up transportation for you."

I nodded, hunched my head down and doubled back across to a ditch alongside the dirt road. One by one, I made my way around to the men of the 2nd platoon and gave them the word. They scattered out and took up positions from which they could lay down a heavy concentration of fire on the enemy up there on the hill. I could hear the "ping" of spent M-1 clips, marking the steady passing of another eight rounds.

The enemy weren't sitting on their hands, of course. The dirt was kicking up all over the place as they banged away. As long as we kept pouring in the lead, though, they'd stay down in their holes long enough to let the rest of the battalion get away.

This was one maneuver we were getting good at. I watched as the GI's pulled back past our positions. Charley company was in the assembly area helping put the wounded on litter jeeps and throwing what gear we had left into the trucks.

The place was a madhouse. The big truck engines were roaring as the drivers gunned them impatiently. And over that din came the constant crack of rifle fire and the frp ... frrp of Commie burp guns.

ONE by one the trucks from the service company rolled out in a cloud of dust and headed south, to positions that were the beginning of the Naktong River line and the Pusan Perimeter. I watched as they pulled away. Finally I yelled at my men to get ready to pull back and hop on the bandwagon. The enemy fire had slackened off some as they watched their quarry get away. I hoped they hadn't realized yet that only my lousy 30-man platoon was left to handle their whole company.

We were back in the woods now and ready to climb aboard the truck as soon as it came tearing up. Suddenly there was a lull in the shooting and I heard it; it meaning nothing. The quiet hurt my ears. There should have been the throaty rumble of a six by six lumbering down the road. But there wasn't. Only silence.

My mouth went a little dry. How were we going to catch up with the rest of Charley company, with no transportation? I stood there stupidly, looking out into the clearing still clouded with the fine powder of the brown Korean dust thrown up by the trucks that had jammed the area just a few minutes ago.

Suddenly the sound of a far-off engine broke the silence. The men relaxed with big silly grins on their faces, laughing at themselves for getting up a sweat about being left behind.

But as the sound of the engine grew louder, it became painfully familiar. It was a jeep-one stinking jeep. It careened around the corner like a hot-rodder down Main Street. It really wasn't rolling, though, it was thumping. Three of its tires were shot flat, the rubber flaying around in ribbons where rifle slugs had chewed it up.

The driver pulled up looking scared green.

"You see a truck back there?" I asked.

The kid at the wheel shook his head. He jerked this thumb back toward the direction of the vehicle park.

"There's one back there, all right. But it's burning. They clobbered it."

So that was it. We had a whole Red division at our backs. Ahead was a no man's land crawling with enemy patrols. And we were left alone.

I turned to face my platoon. We were completely cut off. Anything could happen now, and all of it was bad....

It was only about eight A.M., but we had been in contact with the enemy since well before midnight. Then all three companies of the battalion had gone through the tiny village of Cheri.

It was just another cluster of mud huts in a small valley surrounded by more nameless hills. We burned the village and pushed through it, consolidating our lines on its northern fringe. Baker and Dog companies set up a perimeter defense and my gang of Charley company were in reserve about a hundred yards back.

We had gotten a few hours' sleep when the old man called me over to the CP. With him was the first sergeant, a radio operator, and a couple of runners from the platoons up on the line.

The CO waved his hand in a northerly direction.

"Take your platoon across the river, Stevens," he said. "I figure the enemy is over there in force some place. Find out who the hell they are and what they're up to."

I went back to the area and got the men up. This was going to be a recon patrol. That at least meant we could travel light. The guys that had 'em pulled on fatigue caps. The rest went bareheaded. Steel helmets would make too much noise. Each man had an M-1 but we left the BAR's behind. I shoved a couple extra magazines for my .45 into my belt and we were ready to push out. I wasn't even taking my Thompson submachine gun along on this one.

We moved around our line's left flank and hit the river. It was shallow enough to wade across; we got over without a hitch.

The night was pitch black but still hot and sticky. The "hill" the captain wanted us to use as our observation point seemed to be about the size of Pike's Peak. It was maybe 600 or 700 yards up on a sharp angle. The men sweated and cussed Korea and its rotten little war.

By about 4:30 A.M. we got to the military crest. I took three men to the top and over the forward slope into a position where we could observe the enemy. We sat well concealed in the dense scrub brush and waited. Through the gray overcast, the light finally grew brighter and brighter. And I didn't need much to get a view that made my stomach do flips. There, spread out about four miles away, was the biggest concentration of enemy troops I would ever see. They filled the valley.

None of us talked. We kept our binoculars glued to our eyes and made fast notes on what we saw. I didn't figure on hanging around there for long. I wanted to soak up as much info as possible and then haul out. This wasn't just some assembly area we had below us. The outfit was a big one and ready to move forward. Their tanks were drawn up in battle formation. Trucks were being loaded. I figured this to be at least a full armored division, maybe 15,000 men.

WE saw enough. We pulled back over the top of the hill and down to where the rest of the platoon was waiting. The trick now was to get away without being spotted

We snaked our way down the hill with the daylight getting stronger by the minute. We made good time. Already I could make out our positions back across the river

Then suddenly all hell broke loose over there. Machine guns and rifles cut loose. I saw tracers pulling their red arcs against the dark brown hills. But something was wrong-plenty wrong. The fire was being exchanged between the crest of the hill and its base. But we were supposed to be holding both. Those were our positions. Baker and Dog were supposed to be at the top on the line with Charley down at the bottom. Now, though, the fire was between the two.

I could only guess at the reason; it was a tragically good guess. The enemy had cut around our flank and infiltrated our perimeter. The boys sunk there in their holes were dead tired from the all-day fight. The Reds had slipped in and chopped them up.

I figured we'd be needed badly, so we disregarded the need for quiet and went plunging down the hill. We hit the river and began to wade across it in a line of skirmishers formation. We were just about in the middle when the roof caved in. The mountain at our rear erupted into life. Three hidden Red machine gun nests opened up. They poured direct fire into our platoon line.

I yelled at the men to spread out and get out of the water as fast as they could. But we were sitting ducks. The water churned up into a white fury as the machine gun slugs sent up little geysers all around us.

I turned once and saw one of my men jerk upright. He was hit in the back. Before he fell, a couple more slugs slammed into him. They almost cut the poor kid in half. One of his buddies grabbed his collar and pulled him along through water now red with blood. Those few yards seemed like miles.

A couple minutes later we were on the bank. Medics from C company came running toward us. I saw that two more men were hit, their bodies sprawled up on the muddy gravel shore where they had been pulled.

"Take care of 'em," I shouted, pointing to the three.

The medics made it to them okay, but they stopped their rushing after they bent over them a couple seconds. The sergeant looked up at me.

"What'd you expect us to do, Mac?"

I REPORTED the loss of the three men to the captain and quickly gave him a rundown on what we had found on the other side of the mountain. He couldn't get too interested at the moment. His own positions had been hit and hit hard by a reinforced company. They commanded the heights above us and were dumping a steady stream of lead down into our lines -a lot of it from our own guns.

That's when the old man elected to find greener pastures, and nominated my platoon to cover the retreat.

"You guys have been sitting up there on your tails all night," he said, waving his carbine in the direction of the mountain. "It's about time you did some work."

It wasn't a great joke, but he meant well. I spotted the men around the area and set up a fire field to cover the bug out. The men from the other companies 66 helped by throwing all they had at the enemy from their ring mounted 50 cal. mg's mounted atop the two-and-a-half-ton trucks.

From the other outfits we got another five BAR's and a couple extra air-cooled 30 cal. machine guns. We even jerked one 50 cal. gun from a wrecked jeep to use. The thing didn't have a mount so one of the men rested it in the crotch of a tree and used that for a support.

We kept up enough fire to let the battalion get away. The pull-out went fine until it came time for us to leave. And then we were alone. Twenty-seven men, on foot, miles out in front of the nearest friendly position.

We had no maps, not even a compass. No food and only half-empty canteens.

Well, I figured, the infantry was born to walk. If there was any dying to do, we might as well be on our feet and moving. I told the men to lighten their loads as much as possible and still preserve enough fire-power to defend ourselves.

We yanked the bolts out of all the machine guns and threw 'em away to keep the enemy from using them. Then we strung on our bandoleers of ammo and started hiking-south. The sun boiled down as we slogged along through the underbrush.

This suddenly became a private war, a little one between my platoon and the enemy. Everything was in their favor except one thing: we planned to get back -alive. The enemy had other intentions, and he made them known a couple hours later. We had been pushing on our way, trying to keep out of sight, when we saw a North Korean patrol.

They were coming up toward us from the south. Proof enough that they were all over the place, probing our weak lines. We took cover and waited until they got in close. Then we opened up. Our M-1's spit lead up and down their line. The Reds took the hint. They dove into the bush and disappeared. But I knew we weren't going to be let off so easily.

I was right. Around two P.M. they caught up with us again. This time there were more of them and they banged away at us for almost 20 minutes. We finally got away without casualties. But now we had more trouble.

In fighting off the two enemy units, we had to change our line of march. We had started out originally in a southerly direction, with only five or six miles to cover. But after hiking for almost eight hours, we still hadn't reached anything that looked familiar. There was only one conclusion: we were hopelessly lost.

A cloud cover made figuring direction by the sun impossible. Besides, we had moved up into this area originally at night. As a result, we didn't have a chance to get familiar with terrain features. THE day dragged on. We hadn't eaten, and hiking in the steaming heat left us weak with exhaustion. We pulled up some green peanuts from a field and ate them. At night we dropped to the ground on a hillside and slept, the first rest since the jump-off against Cheri.

The next day was a duplication of the one before. A thin, double line of men, shoulders hunched down under the weight of rifles and ammo, slogging along. It was hard enough to just keep moving. But we had to fight for our lives, too.

Around 10:30 A.M., we were stopped by a large enemy force. We tried to pull back into some woods but they had us. A vicious fire fight hammered on. Two of my men went down. One was dead when I got to him. The other was cut to ribbons and damn near dead, too. I had nothing to give him for the pain that I knew racked his battered body. There was no choice. We had to leave him or get killed trying to bring him along. I prayed to God that I was doing the right thing. We broke contact with the enemy and got away.

Late that afternoon, we stumbled into a tiny Korean village. It was deserted. We went through it looking for food. A couple crocks of kimchi, fermented Korean cabbage, and some rice was all we could find. It wasn't much, but it helped beat down the pangs of hunger.

We stayed there. that night, or most of it, that is. About 2:30 a.m., one of the guards I'd posted woke me up. "Steve," he whispered hoarsely, "they're coming again."

I crawled outside the hut and heard motors. They were the wheezy engines of Russian trucks used by the North Koreans. I got the men up and we crept out and back into the hills.

Each move like this was getting us more and more lost. But there was no choice. The enemy had strong patrols working back and forth parallel to our lines. We had to run and hide like hunted animals, or die.

Daylight finally came, but we still had no idea where we were. We scrounged for rice in deserted farm huts and drank brackish water scooped out from filthy wells. We moved blindly through the hills, circling away from signs of the enemy and, if possible, becoming more and more lost.

That night we slept in the woods, afraid to risk being caught in another village. Dawn of the third day broke with no hope of reaching our lines. Sooner or later we were going to stumble into a large enemy force. Then we'd be too low on ammo and too weak to fight long or effectively. And then this madness would end.

Yet, we still weren't beaten. As long as we had clips for the M-1's and a few handfuls of rice. I was determined to keep the men moving.

At a little before noon, we spotted another enemy patrol. This time we had been moving along the crest of a hill so we saw them first. My men deployed behind rocks and trees and waited for them to get into range, then we opened up. I saw a couple of the enemy riflemen drop under our fire. The rest disappeared in quick time. This puzzled me, though. They easily outnumbered us, and ordinarily the Reds weren't inclined to break off an engagement so quickly, especially when they had numbers on their side.

A REASON for their action came to my mind, but I didn't dare get up any hope. This unit could have been the rear guard of the convoy we saw the day before. They probably wanted to keep up with the main body of their force for one reason: they were near enough to U. N. lines to draw fire!

Even this long shot gave us renewed energy. The men straightened up and moved forward with their heads up now. We headed along the hillside paralleling the road down which the enemy had just come.

We had gone about another mile or so when we heard the distant drone of an engine. This time it was no wheezing Russian truck but the sweet purr of an an airplane. Seconds later we saw it, an Army artillery L-5 cutting low over the hilltops, looking around for likely targets.

The men broke out of cover and stood in the clear, waving their hands and shouting. I had often seen such things in the movies when guys shipwrecked on some desert island went through such antics to attract the attention of a passing ship. I never thought I'd be doing the same thing to a little ol' L-5.

The plane banked low and buzzed us. That put-putting engine made the sweetest music we ever heard, believe me. The pilot wagged the ship's wings. Then he turned and we got the idea: this was the direction in which we should be going.

We stepped off smartly now. An hour and a half later, we saw a patrol from Charley company. They had come out to bring us in. They had a couple of trucks waiting. We climbed aboard and rolled back to our own lines-at last.

The Old Man was standing there in the company area when we pulled up. He flipped a cigarette from his mouth.

"Just where the hell you guys been?" he bellowed at us.

THE END

'I'll Give You the Secrets FREE'

HOW YOU CAN CASH IN ON THE EXPLODING PLASTICS INDUSTRY

Space Technology break-thru has developed new Plastic Materials, Processes and Methods. Now you can Fabricate, Mold, Shape, Laminate and Form new Plastic Materials with hundreds of wanted and needed Glamour Items at HOME! My New, easy-to-learn methods put you in high-profit Plastics Business overnight! Start small—grow big—I'll pave the way for you. Use my money, I'll set you up—help sell your products at good prices, guide you every step of the way and virtually pay you for your Spare Time. Stop wasting Time—get your share of the easy money available now in the BOOMING Plastics Business. HOME PRODUCERS needed desperately everywhere NOW! Send for FREE "No Selling Plan" Booklet and all the complete exciting details of this amazing new Home Business. Learn the hidden secrets of how YOU can cash in quickly on the Exploding Plastics Industry TODAY!

— — — — Air Mail for Quick Reply — — — —

Mr. William (Bud) Williams, Pres.,
Nationwide Plastics Co., Dept............ CC-2
Box 23321, Los Angeles 23, California

I want to make money FAST in my spare time.
Mail me FREE your "NO SELLING PLAN" Booklet.

Name:.. Age..........
Address:..
City:.................................. Zone:......... State:............

Tell us what you think about this issue of **Men's Adventure Reader!**

Go to our Facebook page:
www.facebook.com/groups/maqbrigade

"I've got a price on me, too."

YOU DON'T HAVE TO CARRY A GUN TO BE A PROFESSIONAL CRIME FIGHTER

Enjoy Top Pay, Security as

FINGERPRINT TECHNICIAN

TRAIN AT HOME IN SPARE TIME!

You are needed now to work "behind the scenes" in crime fighting! You can make a fine salary with exceptional job security in the field of Scientific Crime Detection and Fingerprint Identification. You will be part of a professional team that apprehends the vicious criminal by building an airtight case that sends him to jail! You don't carry a gun—you are the vital "inside" man! Your job is exciting and important. With the constant increase in crime, the need for you becomes even more urgent.

I've helped hundreds of ambitious, dedicated men get into Crime Investigation and Fingerprint Identification. I can help you, too! At your home in your spare time I will reveal the many secrets of this exciting profession...Police Photography, Firearms, Handwriting Identification, the art of "Shadowing" and other skills you will be using in daily assignments. Your past experience is not important. Your ambition and will to succeed *ARE* important.

Our graduates are leaders in this vital work. Over 800 Identification Bureaus around the world employ IAS graduates. IAS is accredited by the National Home Study Council. Rush the coupon. We employ no salesmen; everything will be rushed to you by mail. Learn now about this opportunity; decide for yourself if it is right for you. No obligation.

G.I. BILL APPROVED

OVER 800 American Bureaus of Identification employ IAS Graduates

FREE!
Read the famous Blue Book of Crime

Filled with little known crime facts and famous criminal cases. Tells how you can find success and security in Crime Investigation and Fingerprint Identification. Free! Just mail coupon. No salesman will call.

INSTITUTE OF APPLIED SCIENCE
A Correspondence School Founded in 1916
Dept. 3709, 1920 Sunnyside Ave., Chicago, Ill. 60640

CLIP AND MAIL COUPON NOW

INSTITUTE OF APPLIED SCIENCE
Dept. 3709, 1920 Sunnyside Ave., Chicago, Ill. 60640
Send me FREE the latest edition of the Blue Book of Crime and information on opportunities in Crime Detection and Fingerprint Identification.

Name _____ AGE ____
Address _____
City _____ State _____ Zip ____

THE LAST RIDE OF THE REBEL JOY GIRL CAVALRY

By: Chuck McCarthy
Art by: Unknown
From: **MAN'S STORY,** February, 1963

Secesh harlots succumbed to a different kind of lust in their savage attacks on the women-spoiling Bluebacks.

SERGEANT Barnaby Hastings rubbed a hand over his porcupine-like whiskers. He looked from one to the other of his patrol composed of men from the Second Illinois Volunteers. He knew they hated his guts and that made him happy.

"So I see this house on Peachtree Street. There's nothing but secesh women there. You don't have to tell me nothing about secesh women. They got a hankering for a man that makes them turn into alley cats.

"I go up to this one secesh gal. I tell her she's working and she comes padding up the steps after me like a playful puppy. She's built for action and she loves every minute of it. After we get done, she hands me this diamond ring. Guess she never had it so good."

He reached into his cartridge case and withdrew the ring, passing it around the fire. Bill Cooper took it, rolled it over in his massive palm, studied it in the flickering fire light.

"Sure as hell was in a hurry to give it to you, sarge," he said. "Them brown spots are blood, ain't they."

Hastings glared at Cooper. "Okay, so she thought she was too damned good for me. Taught her a lesson she'll never forget. The secesh bitch will never forget she was with a man."

Cooper spat into the flames. He hated the loud-mouthed bastard more than anything else in the world. Hastings had been a tinhorn, a Chicago card sharp who'd been paid to take over the draft call of the scion of an important Northside family. Serving with Sherman's Bummers had meant only one thing to him. It gave him the inalienable right to rape and pillage his way through Atlanta and now north along the trail to Marietta.

At that very moment the secesh girl who'd never forget Hastings was past remembering anything. Her body encased in a plain pine board coffin rested on the tail of a buckboard wagon.

Connie Loring stood beside the wagon, sweat running down her beautiful young face. She leaned heavily on the shovel which had cut its way through the heavy clay soil. She turned to Marie Oglethorpe who held a handkerchief to her reddened eyes.

"Stop that damned sniveling," Connie ordered. "It won't change things one little bit. Let's get on with the service."

Six girls stepped forward. They reached for the box, lifting it to their shoulders and staggered up the hill to the narrow grave. Connie followed them, carrying a worn leather-covered Bible in her graceful hands.

She watched them lowering the coffin into the ground. "Guess I ought to say something over Alice," Connie mused. "Not that there's much to say. She was a good kid and we all loved her and now she's dead and moldering. And we got a score to settle with the bummers. There aren't any men folk left to do it for us. So we'll do it for ourselves."

Thus on 19 October, 1864, the strangest vendetta of the Civil War began. Connie Loring who'd been one of the leading madames in the once affluent heart of the Confederacy rode out into the woods at the head of her joy girl column, searching for the bummers who had snuffed out Alice's life in a senseless and brutal rape. Perhaps if it had been a girl other than Alice, the need to avenge her wouldn't have burned so strongly in Connie's breast. But Alice had been the vivacious and lovely younger sister of Constance Loring.

A bummer had seized Alice while roaring drunk and after having spent his lust with her had strangled her out of sheer cussedness. There was going to be hell to pay. And Connie was going to make sure that it was paid in full.

For weeks the joy girls lay in the woods just north of Atlanta, training themselves in horsemanship and learning how to fire rifles. THE first assault came on the

flank of 4th Massachusetts Volunteers, bivouaced three miles east of Peach Tree Creek.

A lone sentry gasped in amazement at the sight of ten nearly naked women charging bareback into the campfire. Fear that he had never known before immobilized him as Connie wheeled her horse at him, the mount's flailing hooves kicking up a shower of sparks from the flames.

His adversary was at once the most beautiful woman and the most terrible he had ever seen. Her copper colored hair flew in wild disarray behind her. Her magnificent breasts stood out firm and proud against the tight restraint of her camisole.

He threw his arms over his face to blot out the apparition of this she-demon of hate. But Connie's bayonet lanced through his throat, drenching her horse with the man's blood.

Three other members of the squad sought to disentangle themselves from their blankets. They died on the ground where they had slept. In a matter of moments, the Georgia clay was slippery with the blood of Federals.

With a wild cry of triumph, Connie Loring wheeled her dappled roan and led her girle away from the scene of carnage. The blush of victory caused a wild stirring in her heart.

But as she later lay in the farmhouse hideout at Roswell, a mood of depression came over her. At best count seven blue backs had fallen before the savagery of the assault. But they had died quickly. They hadn't suffered the way Alice had. There was no slow cutting off of air, no certainty of death.

Connie called her girls around her. "This is not good enough," she said. "We must take captives."

Seeing the unholy mad light in the beautiful girl's eyes, Eustice Cross felt a sense of dread. "You're beginning to act like an Indian squaw," she argued.

"And who has a better right? Our land has been defiled. They have butchered innocent women. They die too quickly."

Some of the others blanched at the idea of hostages. But they had become used to taking the orders of the headstrong madame.

"We are a military group now and I'm the leader. You'll follow my orders or take the consequences," Connie warned. "From now on, we take prisoners. We bring them back here. Is that understood?"

Eustice looked at Connie long and hard. The younger girl's shoulders finally slumped. "We'll follow you," she answered, speaking for the entire group.

On 25 October, the second raid took place. Stripped nude, the girls rode their horses into a campfire of the 7th Ohio. Swiftly they killed with a fury born of lust. However Corporal Joe Mildown and Private Henry Talbert were not allowed to die swiftly.

Connie's girls surrounded the stunned men and roped them to their horses. The Union soldiers were dragged more than a mile to the deserted farm.

More dead than alive they were thrown into a hayloft. Mildown stared in complete disbelief as Connie rested on one knee beside him. As she held the ever present bayonet to his throat, she stripped the shirt from his bloody body.

The sharp blade of the bayonet sliced through his boot laces. Weak from the loss of blood, he found it impossible to resist Connie as she stripped the last of his clothes from him.

"All right, yankee dog," she whispered with venom. "Amuse me if you want to live."

As Connie lay beside him, her nails raking his chest, her lithe thighs touching his, Mildown heard the blood-curdling cries of Talbert. Indeed, Connie's girls were using a bayonet on him in a manner for which it never was intended.

"You're worse than Commanche squaws!" Mildown groaned. He saw the bayonet poised above his throat.

"That's for Alice, Yankee Bummer!" Connie felt his life's blood gushing hot over her naked breast. She looked down at the dead soldier no longer feeling hatred for him. There was nothing left to hate.

THE following morning a forager 1 patrol from the 32nd New York found two corpses so mutilated that their sex could not be determined. They were buried in a clearing.

The smell of blood had caused unmistakable changes in Connie's girls. Quickly they were turning into predatory she-beasts. Connie understood the reason. No longer was it a matter of vengeance against Sherman's Bummers alone. It was revenge against all men who had used their voluptuous bodies at will and then cast them aside. For the first time in their lives, the women were able to dominate men completely. They reveled in the strangled cries of their tortured victims. They enjoyed hearing them beg for their manhood and at last for their miserable lives.

Connie watched the change, but did nothing to stop it. Some say the loss of her sister had smashed her sanity. One chronicler of the Atlanta Campaign stated: "It must be thought significant that Constance Loring never shed so much as one tear over her murdered sister. Even at the graveside she showed none of the emotion that might be expected to accompany such a loss.

"The fact that she retained her composure and command of herself and her harlots during this most trying period cannot be regarded as entirely normal.

"It can be supposed that every man she first seduced and then kiled represented the murderer. The fact that she took no part in the mutilations either of those who were still alive, or those whom she had already killed with her bayonet indicates that psychologically she had taken on the role of her lamented kin. Something perverse within her motivated her to press her intentions on her captive and at his moment of fulfillment to strike her lethal blow. She killed in much the same way as the black widow spider tears out the heart of her mate."

Unaware that their outposts were systematically being attacked and wiped out by a band of marauding women, the Military Division of the Mississippi placed an incredible price of ten thousand dollars on the heads of the raiders.

News of the bounty was posted by every company command. Fear and avarice combined to make the woods a perilous place for those who walked there. Patrol leaders ordered their men to fire at patrols coming through the woods at them.

If Constance Loring was indeed insane, she had the cunning of a wild animal. Her harlots hit with the lightning thrust of a rapier only to disappear into nothingness until the next raid. Her toll of mutilated bummers grew. She lived now only for the sight of blood.

With grim irony, fate worked inexorably towards a final confrontation between the harlots and Sergeant Barnaby Hastings. Hastings dreamed of nothing so much as the ten thousand dollar price tag which hung on the heads of the unknown rebel raiders.

"I'm going to get them secesh boys and I'm going to skin their carcasses and throw them at Old Tecumseh's feet," he told his squad the night that his request for detached duty was approved. "There's eight of us. That means better than a thousand dollars a man if we bring the Johnny Rebs in. You know how many women I can buy up on State Street for a thousand dollars?"

The plan was simple. The squad had been detached from the Second Illinois Volunteers. It was now free to roam at will, searching out the phantom raiders.

THE rest of the account comes from Private Bill Cooper whose from Private Bill Cooper whose diary gives a graphic description.

"We followed the Etowah River trail to the Oostanaula and then wheeled north towards Lay's Ferry. We made a big show of camping out, building our camp fires until they were as bright as beacons. We thought we were prepared for anything.

"But when the raiders hit, we stood dumbfounded. Can you imagine a group of the most beautiful women you've ever seen, riding out of the trees almost naked? It was enough to stop us in our tracks. We didn't know whether to laugh or shoot until they were on us.

"A horse came at me with flashing hooves. Instinctively, I reached up to dismount the rider. My hand touched a thigh that felt like velvet. The girl beat at me with a bayonet, cutting my hands severely. I held on for all I was worth, dragging her from the saddle.

"There were cries all around me as the girl and I rolled in the mud. Her knees jammed up into my groin and I went weak all over. Still I held on. I finally managed to roll over and sit astride her, feeling the luscious softness of her body under me. I seized both her wrists and held them at arm's length over her head. She lay beneath me spitting curses. I thought that if she had been a man I would have picked up the nearest rock and bashed her brains out.

"But the raider wasn't a man. She was easily the most devastatingly lovely girl I'd ever seen. I hesitated for the slightest instant. That was all they needed. Pain blasted through the back of my head.

"The next thing I knew, I came to, finding myself being dragged over the rough trail by a lariat which was attached to the girl's saddle horn. Rough stones cut my shirt to ribbons. My arms felt as if they were being torn from their joints. I closed my eyes and prayed like I'd never done before.

"At last we reached a farm house. For the first time I realized that I hadn't been the only survivor of the raid. They dragged Barnaby Hastings in after me. He was cut and bleeding and breathing defiance.

"'I'll be eternally damned!'" he yelled. 'A platoon of strumpets. Stand back and give me time, ladies. I'll take care of you all. I know what you secesh girls need. And Barnaby Hastings is the man to give it to you.'

"The copper haired one wielded her bayonet like a whip. I saw her turn up the wick in a lamp she carried. She walked around Hastings, examining him as if he were a prize steer. I saw her bayonet flash in the lamplight and heard Hastings scream. For a moment, I thought she had butchered him right then and there.

"Hastings bent double. She had hit him across the belly with the flat side of her bayonet. The others paid little attention to me, feeling I was still to weak to try to escape. Every one of them had their eyes fixed on Hastings. They prodded him with their bayonets, forcing him to his knees. Then they stood back.

"They motioned to the girl who was obviously their leader. "Take him, Connie,' they said.

"I couldn't believe what happened next. The woman called Connie sank down beside Hastings and cupped his face in her hands. She watched as one of the others dug a bayonet into the base of his spine. Hastings couldn't hold back the howl of protest.

"Maybe I should have felt sorry for him, but if any one of us deserved this kind of treatment, he did.

" 'I'll give you anything. Just let me go! he whined. He pushed the diamond ring he had shown us into Connie's hands. She turned it over in her fingers, studying it in the lamp's flicker. A look I had never seen in a woman before came into her eyes.

"The Rebel girl shrugged out of what was left of her clothing and sat on her haunches regarding Hastings.

"So you're man enough for a secesh girl,' she taunted him. 'Prove it!'

"The others stood around watching. They didn't giggle or turn away. They were transfixed by the sight of the girl and the soldier. I couldn't understand it.

"I thought about escaping through the barn door, but it had been bolted securely.

"When it was over, Hastings looked up pleading. All he saw was a ring of steel closing in on him. The woman called Connie hurled the ring in his face.

" "This is all you give me of my sister, bummer. Then join her in hell!' she cried.

"She set the lamp down beside him. She kept licking her lips with her tongue. The others surrounded Hastings. Everywhere he turned, there was another knife ready to slice him.

"At that moment, I spied a small - window on the side wall of the barn. Hastings' screams of agony covered whatever little noise I made as I crawled to it.

"I managed to straddle the sill. As I looked back, they were literally cutting Hastings apart on the floor. His torso was one bloody gash. He screamed continuously, not even pausing for breath.

"His bare legs thrashed out. One of them caught the oil lamp and sent it spinning into the hay. "Instantly a long plume of smoke towards the loft. A dull orange glow lit the barn as I jumped to safety.

"I ran wildly into the woods as if I were being chased by the hounds of hell. The screams which came from the barn were like nothing of this earth. Roaring flames crackled through the night.

" 'Have mercy on them all!' I prayed as I ran.

"The following morning I returned to the Second Illinois Volunteers. I reported as lone survivor of the detached patrol. I told my commanding officer that we had been bushwhacked by superior forces and that Barnaby Hastings had died fighting the enemy in a barn. I just couldn't bring myself to recite the horrible details of what I had seen in the slaughter house."

So ended the diary of Bill Cooper and the lives of Connie Loring and her wild, man-killing harlots.

THE END

"Sure he's a police decoy, but he's the last woman I remember!"

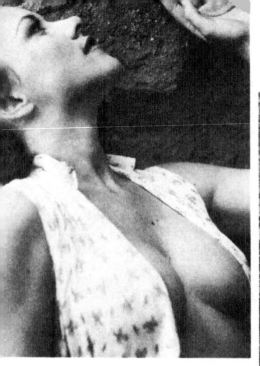

DAWN RICHARDS

But Dawn is mercurial, quick to change . . . here—and then gone. An all-too-brief glimpse of loveliness for those of us privileged to see her. And it is a rare privilege—and an even rarer pleasure.

Beverly's ready wit and winning charm have made her the darling of Miami's leading lens men.

Issue #1: Westerns
Gunsmoke, Juli Reding

Issue #2: Espionage
The Jane Bonds

Issue #3: Vigilante Justice
Executioner 2 Book Bonus

Issue #4: Jungle Girls
Jane Dolinger

Issue #5: Dirty Missions
Eva Lynd, Norm Eastman

Be sure and order your copies today!

Available worldwide
on amazon
or direct from us at
www.menspulpmags.com

Printed in Great Britain
by Amazon